What

"Did you say *psychic?*" Dane's dark brows drew together as he took his gaze from the road and looked at the woman sitting next to him in the pickup. "Exactly what did you do to get in such a mess?"

Kara drew a ragged breath and tried to collect her thoughts. His question wasn't easy to answer. "I came because of the horses."

"You're in Tijuana to talk to horses? Right."

"Not to *talk* to them. To decide which ones are going to win."

"You were fixing races? Lady, no wonder someone's mad at you." And no wonder she had been running away and ended up hiding in *his* truck!

RITA RAINVILLE

grew up reading truckloads of romances and replotting the endings of sad movies. She had always wanted to write the kind of romances she likes to read. She finds people endlessly interesting and that is reflected in her writing. She is happily married and lives in California with her family.

Dear Reader,

Although our culture is always changing, the desire to love and be loved is a constant in every woman's heart. Silhouette Romances reflect that desire, sweeping you away with books that will make you laugh and cry, poignant stories that will move you time and time again.

This summer we're featuring Romances with a playful twist. Remember those fun-loving heroines who always manage to get themselves into tricky predicaments? You'll enjoy reading about their escapades in Silhouette Romances by Brittany Young, Debbie Macomber, Annette Broadrick and Rita Rainville.

We're also publishing Romances by many of your all-time favorites such as Ginna Gray, Dixie Browning, Laurie Paige and Joan Hohl. Your overwhelming reaction to these authors has served as a touchstone for us, and we're pleased to bring you more books with Silhouette's distinctive medley of charm, wit and—above all—*romance*. I hope you enjoy this book, and the many stories to come.

Sincerely,

Rosalind Noonan
Editor
SILHOUETTE BOOKS

SRRL-7/85

RITA RAINVILLE
Lady
Moonlight

Silhouette *Romance*

Published by Silhouette Books New York

America's Publisher of Contemporary Romance

Silhouette Books by Rita Rainville

Challenge the Devil (ROM #313)
McCade's Woman (ROM #346)
Lady Moonlight (ROM #370)

SILHOUETTE BOOKS
300 E. 42nd St., New York, N.Y. 10017

ISBN: 0-373-08370-X

First Silhouette Books printing July, 1985

10 9 8 7 6 5 4 3 2 1

To the special men in my life--

Don, my husband
Paul and Steve, our sons
David, my brother, and
Jim, John, and Tom, my nephews

and

Ken and Gini Robinson,
who shared their bit of Baja
and "gave" me an orphanage.

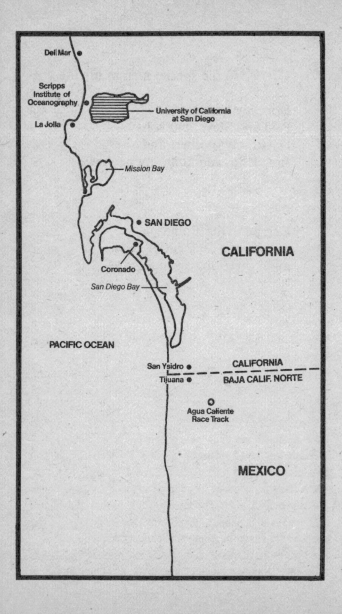

Chapter One

"Did you say *psychic?*" Dane Logan's dark brows drew together as he took his eyes from the road and looked at the rumpled bit of feminity lying on the seat beside him.

"Well, semi," Kara Brady said after a moment, feeling that the situation called for scrupulous honesty.

"As a semipsychic, exactly what did you do to get in such a mess?"

With her head pressing against his hard thigh and her silvery-blond hair sliding like silk over his jeans, Kara drew in a ragged breath and tried to collect her scattered thoughts. His sardonic question wasn't all that easy to answer. At least, not starting in the middle. "I came because of the horses."

"You're in Tijuana to talk to horses? Right." His mild tone was in savage contrast to the way he shifted gears and steered the high-powered pickup forward a few feet.

"Not to *talk* to them." Kara spoke shortly, annoyed at his obtuseness. "To decide which ones are going to win the races."

"You were at Caliente," he said, nodding back in the direction of the racetrack, "fixing races? Lady, no wonder someone's mad at you."

"Of course not!" She lifted her head in indignation, only to have a hard hand push it back down. "I don't do things like that. I wouldn't know how, even if I wanted to," she added with her usual candor.

Dane scowled at the bumper-to-bumper line of cars stretched out before him. "Lady, we're about a hundred feet from the checkout point. Before we get there you either convince me that you're not involved in anything illegal or you get tossed out on your cute little butt to fight your own battle."

What had possessed him to interfere? he wondered once again. His normal mode of operation was to ignore what didn't strictly concern him. At least, across the border. It wasn't healthy to become embroiled in someone else's arguments, he reminded himself. Especially across the border.

But this had been different. He had just returned to the truck and started the motor, checking automatically for kamikaze drivers, when she rounded the corner. It hadn't been just her platinum-blond hair that caught his eye. It wasn't even the nicely distributed curves so obvious beneath the white, full-skirted sundress. Nor the long, shapely legs that obviously had collected their share of appreciation. It was her look of sheer, utter panic, the heavy thudding of footsteps, and the shouted commands of various male voices that followed behind her.

He had reacted instinctively. Throwing open the door on the passenger side, he'd snapped, "Get in!"

Kara shifted restively. How on earth could she explain in such a short time? If he believed her, he would help. If he didn't . . . She shuddered at the thought. She didn't question her own implicit trust. From the moment he had ordered her into the big brown truck, she'd had but one thought: to drop the whole miserable mess into his capable hands. His tone of voice had convinced her that he was accustomed to issuing orders and having them followed without question.

Fine. Let him do just that and get her out of here! The same way he had slammed the door behind her after she'd tossed her purse in the cab and scrambled up after it. The same way he had pushed her down on the seat and told her to be quiet and stay out of sight. The same way he had leisurely set the truck in motion, turning a series of corners and losing the clutch of men so hot to catch up with her.

Now, after leaving the Agua Caliente Racetrack behind, after traversing the raucous mercantilism of Avenida Revolución, as he drew the large truck into the surprisingly short line of cars waiting to go through Customs, he was ready to listen.

"It was the orphanage," she mumbled to his leg, and she felt it jerk in surprise.

"How did orphans get mixed up with a fixed race?" he asked dryly.

"Not fixed," she insisted. "It's perfectly legal." Looking at his jeans-covered kneecap had its disadvantages, she realized. As his voice didn't give away much, seeing his expression might help. "My friends run an orphanage down here. When they're out of money I come down and we go to the races."

"Isn't it risky gambling with the last of their money?"

"That's what I'm trying to tell you. There's no risk at all. I always know which horse is going to win."

"Why don't you just phone them? It'd be quicker, and from what I've seen, a hell of a lot less hazardous." After a moment's thought, he asked, "Who was after you? Do you even know that?"

Kara twisted her head, trying to get a look at her benefactor. Her quick dive into the truck had been made on the basis of a thoroughly Anglo-Saxon voice with the bite of a Marine drill sergeant. She wondered if the man's features were any softer. A muscular forearm, liberally sprinkled with dark brown hair, was so close to her nose that she was all but cross-eyed as she stared at it. Nothing soft there, she decided gloomily. If the rest of him matched the arm and hard thigh she was resting on, she was in trouble. Big trouble.

"You have about five minutes before we reach Customs." Dane's words indicated mild impatience as he looked out over the late Saturday afternoon traffic. The lanes were less congested than usual with motorists returning to the United States from Baja California. "You'd better talk fast."

"Juanito said they were probably professional gamblers. He noticed them watching as he went to collect his winnings. He said—"

"Juanito?"

"My friend. He and his wife, Carmella, are the ones who run the orphanage. We try to be inconspicuous, but Juanito is so big he always attracts attention. After the first three races, he said those guys were watching us like vultures. From then on, the three of us took turns collecting the winnings. By the sixth race, we had enough money. We decided to leave, and they followed us out." Kara gestured expansively with an arm as she explained, only to have her wrist manacled by strong fingers and returned to her side.

"Keep still," he warned laconically. "Your friends must have found transportation. They're outside walking up and down looking into car windows."

"Juanito?" Kara asked eagerly, lifting her head despite the reminder.

"No. The ones who were chasing you."

"Oh."

Dane was momentarily distracted by her softness as she dropped back down. Uh-uh, he warned himself. What you have on your hands—or in your lap, he amended silently—is a genuine, twenty-four karat weirdo. Get her across the border and turn her loose. He had a momentary vision of a hummingbird, flitting and darting, hovering and then, faster than the blink of an eye, disappearing. "So then what happened?" he asked, prodding both himself and the blonde.

"We decided to split up and take off in three different directions. You know, the old divide and conquer theory."

"You mean the bunch that was hot on your heels was only a third of them?"

"No." Wry humor laced the strung-out word. "It didn't work quite the way we planned. We divided, but they almost conquered. They all took off after me, and I panicked. After zigging up one road and zagging down another, I lost all sense of direction. I don't know what they wanted, but they didn't look very friendly. By the time you came along I was fading fast. I don't know how I can ever thank you," she ended breathlessly.

"You might start by telling me the truth."

"I am!" Kara stared at his knee in frustration. How on earth could she explain something so strange that *she* still had trouble believing it? Aunt Tillie had warned her that it would be this way. And she had learned quickly enough not to talk about it. Only Judy and a few close friends knew, and even they thought it was weird. As far as that went, so did she.

"You're not going to believe me," she mumbled pessimistically.

"Try me."

The terse words, uttered in a deep, dry voice, were anything but encouraging, Kara noted dismally. "About a year ago I was at the racetrack at Del Mar with some friends." The words came slowly as she organized her thoughts. "None of us knew much about racing. We made our choices for crazy reasons. You know, things like the horse had a silly name or we liked the colors of the jockey's silks. I picked the winner of every race."

She rushed on as he took a deep breath. "I know

what you're going to say. That it was a fluke. We all thought so. We called it beginner's luck and had a marvelous day. I didn't think anything more about it until I talked to Aunt Tillie. She said that's how it started with her."

"Who's Aunt Tillie? And I warn you," he said softly, his patience visibly strained, "that I'll probably strangle you if you tell me she's your aunt. And what the hell does she have to do with all this?"

Kara twisted, reaching down to straighten her skirt. This man, she thought, in addition to being curt and impatient, was hard to please. What did he want her to say, that Aunt Tillie was her grandmother? "Uh . . . she's actually my great-aunt, my mother's aunt. And she has everything to do with it. She's the one who explained that it runs in the family, but it skips a generation. Now I've got it," she observed gloomily for all the world as if she were announcing that she had broken out in measles.

"Got what?" he asked between clenched teeth.

She sighed in exasperation. "Haven't you been listening? Psychic power!"

"Are we back to that again?"

"We've never left it. You asked me to explain and that's what I've been trying to do. And, to answer your earlier question, I didn't call Juanito because it doesn't work over the telephone. At least, not yet. I have to be at the racetrack. I've tried using a program and a racing form, but nothing happens unless I'm at the track."

Intrigued despite himself, he asked, "When you're there how do you pick a winner?"

"It sounds crazy," she warned.

"You can say that again," he muttered.

Ignoring him, Kara continued. "I just look at the names of the horses running, and I know."

"Woman's intuition?" He didn't try to hide his skepticism.

"No," she said after a moment's serious thought. "It's more than that. It's hard to describe, but a feeling of absolute certainty comes over me. I just *know*."

"How convenient. You must have collected a tidy little nest egg this last year." His thigh muscles tightened as he eased the truck forward.

"Oh, no." She shook her head, bumping it on the steering wheel. "I never bet for myself. Aunt Tillie says even though it's a mixed blessing, it's a gift from God and shouldn't be abused. I'm not sure that she's right, but I don't have a better explanation, so I don't mess around with it. I only use it in emergencies, to help other people."

The air conditioner was loud in the sudden silence, blanketing out the pleas of the roadside vendors taking one last crack at the tourists. The afternoon sun blasted through the windows, and Kara was grateful for the cool stream of air. Dane's sigh, which sounded more like a snort, made her jump.

"Okay, lady. You win."

"You mean you believe me?"

"Let's say that I think *you* believe what you're saying."

"But you really think I'm something out of the loony bin, don't you?"

"You said it, lady, not me."

"Well, right now I'll even settle for that as long as you get me back on U.S. soil."

"Okay. We're getting close. Just pretend you're asleep. I'll cover for you if they say anything as we go through Customs."

Two minutes later, they were across the border, in the town of San Ysidro, and driving north on I-5 to San Diego. Kara had never heard a sweeter sound than that of the powerful motor picking up speed.

Dane's large hand was removed from her head. "Okay, you can sit up now."

He watched her scoot over, fumble with the seat belt and reach for her purse. Her hair had come loose from whatever arrangement it had been in and now cascaded down to her shoulders. Wispy tendrils of ash-gold curls clung to her cheeks and forehead. Another quick, encompassing glance took in a heart-shaped face with a pointed chin and wide-set eyes so dark they seemed black. They were framed by thick brown lashes and brows. Cute, he thought. Crazy as a bedbug, but cute. And young.

His foot eased up on the gas pedal as he turned back to her. "I just thought of something. Are we leaving your car behind?"

"No," she replied absently. "It's parked at the Amtrak depot. I took the trolley down to the border." Trying not to stare, she noted that his profile was as unyielding as his voice. So was everything else. If he were being cast in a movie, she thought whimsically, it would be as a mercenary, called in to single-handedly quell an uprising.

It wasn't just a macho pose. It went far beyond that, she decided, continuing her assessment. He was tall, about six feet, and every inch looked hard, tough and capable. His face was all planes and angles. Not handsome, but fascinating, if you liked the type. Not that she did, she assured herself. She didn't like anything about him. Not his wavy, coffee-brown hair that was brushed back and obviously knew better than to fall forward, not his mustache, even if it was well-trimmed, not even his burnished, dark skin that proclaimed in a no-nonsense way that his waking hours were spent in the sun. And not, mind you, sybaritically lounging by a pool or near the lapping waves of the ocean. No indeed, he would be vigorously burning up calories and sweating. Nope, she agreed with herself, definitely not her type.

Maybe she could introduce him to Judy, she thought, biting back a grin. Her partner, and best friend, had always admired masterful men. She would have been a pushover in the days when men snapped their fingers and expected women to drop at their feet.

"I beg your pardon?" Kara was aware that, in her fanciful meandering, she had missed something.

"I just asked if you weren't a little young to be wandering around alone in T.J."

"No." She kept her answer deliberately brief, hoping to discourage the lecture she could see forming on his lips. For some unfathomable reason, most men took one look at her five-foot-three-inch frame and thought *cute*. They then equated cute with young and assumed she still had a ten o'clock curfew. For someone who had just celebrated her twenty-fifth birthday it was a bit aggravating. Closing her eyes in resignation, she leaned back, resting her head against the seat.

"Do your parents know where you are?" he asked sharply.

"No." She had her own town house and her parents, enjoying their empty nest, checked in with her when they returned from their various jaunts. "If you had a daughter my age, do you think she'd tell you where she was going every time she stepped out the door?"

"You damn well better believe that she'd know not to go across the border, or anywhere else, without my permission." Her silence provoked him. "And she wouldn't find herself being chased by two-bit hoods in a foreign country. Or having to trust a perfect stranger to help her out."

"Surely not perfect," Kara murmured. Her long lashes lifted in time for her to see his lean fingers squeeze the steering wheel until his knuckles whitened. She had no doubt that he visualized his large hands wrapped around her slim, tan throat.

"I'm sorry." She strove for a properly repentant tone, wondering at the same time why he annoyed her so. "You didn't deserve that." For the first time he lifted his gaze from the road and turned to face her. His eyes were silvery green, she noted in surprise. She had expected them to be dark, to match the rest of him.

"I really do appreciate the way you helped me, but I'm older than I look. Really," she insisted in the face of his obvious skepticism. "I've been on my own for some time now."

"And what about the rest of your story?" His eyes were back on the road. His voice informed her that he wouldn't be surprised if she shouted "April Fool!" and broke into insane laughter.

"All true, every word of it." She sighed in exasperation at his quick glance of disbelief. "You don't know how tired I am of trying to explain the inexplicable. Anyway, we've never had trouble before, and I doubt if we ever will again."

"Wait a minute. You're not telling me that you're actually going back there, are you?"

"Well, of course!" Kara shifted her gaze from the traffic, which was thickening as they neared the center of town, to the angry man beside her. What on earth was the matter with him now? "In about a month they'll need money again," she explained matter-of-factly.

"And that's all it takes? Someone yells for help, and you go running?"

"Of course. Isn't that what friends are for?"

"Not my friends."

"You helped me," she pointed out.

"That was different."

"How?"

"You were a woman, alone and in trouble."

"You mean if a man you knew—"

"Right now we're talking about you," he interrupted briskly. "How many people do you do this horse racing thing for?"

"On a regular basis, only Juanito and Carmella. But there have been a few individual cases, strictly one-time things. Like my friend, Molly. Her husband left her. She had no job, no insurance, nothing. Bobby, her little boy, was in an accident, and she didn't have the money to get him out of the hospital. So we went to the races. A few things like that."

"I don't believe it," he muttered. "In case you haven't heard, there's a word for people like you."

Knowing she would hate herself for asking, she bit anyway. "What?"

"A patsy."

They were still arguing as he drove into the Amtrak parking lot. She directed him to her green Camaro and opened the door as he pulled up beside it.

"I won't say it's been fun," she said, taking one last look at his hard, unsmiling face before she stepped down. "But I do thank you for the rescue." She slammed the door and grinned up at him. "I'll pass your favor on to the next unfortunate soul I meet."

She stepped back, undaunted by his glare, waving as he drove out of the parking lot. And that, she thought, is that. At least she wasn't adding a permanent member to the growing number who disapproved of her life-style. He was only a temporary critic. Putting her car in gear, she headed for her home, her work and her friends in La Jolla.

Thirty minutes later, she walked through the door of Cachet, the craft shop that had metamorphosed into one of the town's most distinctive gift boutiques.

"Thank God you're back!" Kara found herself almost smothered by Judy's impulsive hug. Her normally unflappable friend looked suspiciously bright-eyed. Her black hair, usually drawn back in a smooth knot, hung in wisps around her face, and her lipstick looked as if it had been slowly and methodically chewed off.

"I told you I'd be back about four. I'm only a few minutes late."

Judy eyed her grimly. "Don't pull that innocent act with me. Juanito has been burning up the telephone lines for the last hour, and you know how he is when he gets excited. What I managed to understand I didn't like. He was babbling something about *pistoleros,* and that you had disappeared. Why were gangsters chasing you, and where did you go?"

Kara mentally heaped curses upon the head of the absent Juanito as she put her arm around her distraught friend. "Beth," she called to the college student who helped in the store on weekends, "can you take over for a while? We're going to be in the back."

"Sure thing, Kara." A tall, slim girl with brown hair turned away from the blown-glass creations she was dusting. "Take your time. I'll sing out if it gets busy."

"I told you this crazy stuff was going to get you in trouble." Judy eyed Kara darkly as she herded her into the corner of the stockroom they had furnished as an office. "Are you going to listen to me now? No, of course you won't," she answered herself bitterly. "You'll keep running down there doing your crystal-ball routine until everyone at the racetrack knows what you're up to."

She dropped down into a wicker chair, scowled at Kara, who sat across from her, and plowed on without coming up for air. "Don't you understand that there are people who would do *anything* to get the information you conjure up? Doesn't it worry you at all?"

Experience had taught Kara to sit quietly and

listen. Or at least *look* like she was paying attention. Why was it, she wondered for the hundredth time, that almost everyone who knew her tried to organize her life? It must go back to that *cute* thing, she pondered. They took one look at her and decided that she didn't have a brain large enough for two thoughts to rub together.

It wasn't as if she were mentally deficient, she thought, as Judy's words flowed over her. Quite the contrary. Under her optimistic and humorous approach to life she was actually pretty levelheaded. Only a few people, however, were discerning enough to detect the intelligence that was an integral part of her makeup. Judy knew, but at times such as these she tended to forget.

She was beginning to run down, Kara noted with relief. She was now in the you've-got-to-get-rid-of-this-Florence-Nightingale-complex stage.

"You can't keep running around putting Band-Aids on the whole world, Kara. What would happen to these people if you weren't around? They'd survive, that's what. You can't take the whole world on as your personal charity." Judy leaned back, wondering if this time she had said the magic words that would make Kara less vulnerable to appeals for help. As her friend's husky voice reached her ears, she knew that once again she had failed.

"I haven't adopted the whole world, Judy. Only a small part of my neighborhood." Kara shifted to a more comfortable position. "And I am discriminating, you have to give me that. I never take on anyone who's lazy or incompetent. Only those who are hard-working, but for some reason temporarily unable to help themselves."

"What's so temporary about the Estradas? I don't see them working to the point of self-sufficiency. Their reputation is spreading, and every week they find at least one more kid sitting on their doorstep. Pretty soon they'll have to open another place, and then you'll be down there *twice* a month."

Kara grinned. Judy wasn't nearly as tough as she sounded. Once, just once, she had crossed the border to help at the orphanage. She had spent the day hugging babies, playing with the older children and fighting tears. Ever since, she had been playing shamelessly on the heartstrings of friends and business associates, wangling large and small donations for the children. She also spent hours at rummage and garage sales, buying good used clothing with the money. She never worried about sizes. Every item would be put to use. She also never went back.

Kara sighed. "We've been talking about that. We're all concerned about how fast they're growing. We either start going to the dog races at Caliente during the week, in addition to the horses, or come up with something new. I've been thinking about some of your rich friends, the ones who own businesses. Maybe they'd like to adopt an orphanage or sponsor a few of the kids. With all the wealth in this town, we should be able to come up with something. Why don't you ask Bill, your CPA friend, if a charity in another country is tax deductible." Kara stood up. "Let me know what you find out."

Before she could move, Judy pointed a stern finger

at the empty chair. "Sit, Kara! You're not walking out of here until you tell me what happened this afternoon."

Kara flopped back down, scowling hideously at her friend. "You sound just like the man who rescued me. Nag, nag, nag."

"Then he's a man after my own heart," Judy assured her. "Now talk."

Kara heaved a sigh and launched into an imaginative and well-edited version of the day's activities. ". . . then he drove me to my car and left me. If I'm lucky, it's the last I'll ever see of him."

"Was he that bad?"

"Yes."

"What's his name?"

"I don't know. He was too busy telling me what he thought of my antipoverty program to answer any questions."

"What'd he look like?"

Kara grinned. Trust Judy to get right to the heart of the matter. "He's just your type. You'd love him."

"Meaning you didn't." Judy had more than once expressed her opinion of Kara's penchant for quiet, understated men.

"Precisely. He's big, tough, has go-to-hell green eyes and manners to match. He reminded me of Charles Bronson in that movie you made me watch on TV last week."

"And you didn't get his *name?*" Judy regarded her friend through blue eyes round with shock. She didn't believe in passing up heaven-sent opportunities.

"Listen to me," Kara urged. "By the time we reached the depot we could hardly wait to say good-bye. And since we argued all the way from the border, neither of us was in the mood for polite introductions. He's a hard man, and he thinks I'm soft in the head."

She rose, stretched and looked down at the desk they shared. "Sorry I couldn't bring him home for you," she finished absently, picking up a letter. "You'll just have to manage with the ten or so you have hovering around." She looked up, flourishing the letter. "What are we going to do about this?"

"The Business Association charity thing? We'll go, of course. I've already sent them a check. We haven't missed one yet. It's a good cause, and if we need other reasons, we've made some good local connections in the past, and it's tax deductible."

"What more could we ask for?" Kara queried lightly. "What are you going to wear? Something severe, to remind people that you're the brains of the outfit?"

Judy stood up, looking down at Kara from her five-inch advantage. "Sure," she agreed. "As long as your dress is some romantic bit of fluff. God forbid that anyone should think I'm the artistic one," she said piously.

Harmony restored, they turned toward the door. Judy stopped, gesturing dramatically. "Wait a minute! I bet if you really concentrated, you could remember his license number. Then maybe you could track him down through the DMV. What do you think?"

"I think it's a rotten idea," Kara said dryly. "I'm not about to try. I don't want to know his license number; I don't want to know *him*. With luck, I'll never see the man again."

But luck, elusive and unreliable at the best of times, was not with Kara.

Chapter Two

Just one week and a few hours later, she and Judy were being welcomed to a rambling house perched on the cliffs above the Pacific. Judy was in a black-and-white, hip-hugging chemise that was a perfect foil for her dark hair and honey-tanned skin. Kara had chosen a graceful ice-pink dress of crystal-pleated georgette with a wide, square neck and full sleeves ending in deep cuffs. It fell in a soft sheathe to just below her knees.

Dane Logan, lounging near an open window listening to the muted roar of the ocean, stiffened in surprise and watched as Kara turned at the sound of a familiar voice. With a warm smile, she joined a tall, bony man with bright blue eyes. Reaching up, she tugged lightly at a strand of brown hair that drooped over one eye.

"Gary, I think it's time to invite you over for a home-cooked meal again," she said, eyeing him critically.

"I knew my fatal charm would get to you someday," he said calmly.

"Right," she agreed. "Aside from that, no one else can keep my ferns and fuchsias looking the way you do."

"So it's really my green thumb that you love."

She stretched up to give him a quick hug. "Among other things." They grinned at each other, then parted as someone else called her.

Managing to keep well behind her, Dane followed as Kara made her way from one room to another. He watched her meditatively. The poised beauty before him was a far cry from the hoyden who had tumbled into his truck. Her silvery hair was arranged in a graceful swirl that seemed to have no visible means of support. And she was no kid.

Kara was stopped every few feet either to greet friends or acknowledge an introduction. Her natural ebullience drew others like bees to honey. The sound of her husky laughter drifted to him, as someone described an amusing incident.

Judy, who had taken an alternate route, met Kara near a spreading green plant that would have intimidated a normal-size room. "Don't look behind you," she murmured, turning to admire large, shiny green leaves, "but someone dark and determined has been following you since we got here."

Obediently not looking over her shoulder, Kara stared straight ahead into a mirror and met a silvery-green gaze. "Oh, Lord," she murmured, closing her eyes, hoping the apparition would fade before she opened them.

When she did, and it hadn't, she turned to Judy. "Let me introduce you," she said brightly.

"Your rescuer?" The question was redundant. Kara's description had been remarkably graphic.

"Um-hmm."

"You don't know his name, remember?"

"I'll find out! I'll bring him over," she decided, avoiding the mirror, "and—"

"Don't bother," Judy said in amusement. "He's saving you the trouble. He's on his way."

"Terrific," was Kara's weak response. She grabbed her friend's arm. "Remember what I said," she ordered. "He's just your type. You'll be crazy about him!"

"Kara, we both know the kind of men I like, but that one is too much of a good thing. Besides, he's looked right through me several times, and he still doesn't know I'm in the room." She edged away with a grin, forcing Kara to drop her hand. "But he's been eyeing you like a hungry lion who's just found a juicy chunk of meat. I'm removing myself from the line of fire, but I expect a full report on Monday."

"Some friend," Kara mumbled to the space Judy no longer occupied. Oh, come on, she lectured herself in the instant before she turned to face him. It won't be that bad. You say hello; he says hello. You make a clever remark about the incident last week, and he smiles. You thank him again; he nods. You say good-bye, so does he, and that's it. She mustered up a smile and turned.

"Hello."

He looked down, resisting the temptation to touch her hair and see if it was as baby soft as it looked. Instead, he asked, "Are you about ready to eat?"

"What?" She might have known he wouldn't follow a script, she told herself in resignation.

"Are you hungry?"

She nodded. "I'm starved. I haven't eaten since this morning."

"Neither have I. Will you have dinner with me?"

So much for Judy's interpretation of his hungry look, she thought. "You mean, sit with you?" she asked, aware that a lavish buffet was being set up in the next room.

"It's customary."

The man is a complete enigma, she decided, puzzling over his comment. Her response was polite and untruthful. "Thank you, that'll be nice."

"Good. Let's go." One large hand touched the small of her back and nudged her toward the door.

"We're walking away from the food," she pointed out.

"I wasn't talking about salads made from whipped cream, tissue-thin slices of ham, and funny meatballs the size of grapes. I want a steak. Big and thick and rare."

"You mean at a restaurant?" She dug her high heels into the deep pile of the rug and stopped.

"Bright girl." The slight pressure of his hand increased, urging her forward. She halted again as the door closed behind her. *"Now* what's the matter?" he asked, when she wouldn't budge.

She backed up against the house, arms folded

across her chest. "I'm not going. I don't even know your name. A perfect stranger hauls me out of a house and expects—"

He propped a large hand on the wall behind her, just a few inches above her shoulder, and rested his weight on it. His mustache twitched. "I have it on good authority that I'm not perfect."

"You'd better watch it," she warned. "In a minute you're going to break down and smile."

"Dane Logan's the name. Apparently we both own businesses in La Jolla. Can we eat now, or do you need a formal introduction?"

"We eat," she said impulsively as her stomach rumbled. "Where's your car?"

They walked down the curving street past an unself-conscious array of cars ranging from small, economy models to discreet and blatant symbols of wealth. Dane stopped and opened the door of a sleek, black Porsche. As he walked around to his side, Kara wondered fancifully which of his vehicles most truly exemplified the man. The slim, darting and deadly rapier, or the slashing strength of the broadsword?

Before putting the car in gear, he turned to her and asked, "Do I guess, or do you tell me? There is such a thing as reciprocity, you know." At her questioning look he said, "Your name."

"Ah." Buckling her seat belt, she said concisely, "Kara Brady. Born and raised in La Jolla. Twenty-five, single and part owner of Cachet, world-famous gift shop."

Dane checked the rearview mirror and pulled neatly out of the parking space. "World famous?"

"Will you settle for locally renowned?" He nodded,

slowing as he approached a steep curve. "The ball's back in your court. Time for more reciprocity," she informed him, savoring the word.

He concentrated on the traffic, eventually turning onto La Jolla Boulevard before he replied. "I've lived in a lot of places, recently settled here. I'm thirty-three and a contractor."

"You left out the part about being single, engaged or involved," she prompted.

"Is it important?"

"Yes, because I only go out to dinner with men in the first category."

"Which leaves intriguing possibilities for the other two."

"Tonight's invitation," she reminded him as he slid neatly into a parking slot behind the restaurant, "was for dinner. Nothing else, intriguing or otherwise." He walked around the car and opened her door. She looked up, not moving. "Single?" she prodded.

"Single," he agreed absently, reaching for her hand.

Later, watching him demolish his steak as she greedily downed her teriyaki chicken, she decided that he was more than an enigma. His preferred modes of transportation, at least the ones she had witnessed, were poles apart. Reflecting on that at length brought her to the conclusion that there *was* a common denominator—power. And just look at his clothes, she prodded herself. An ebony blazer made of soft, supple suede, gray slacks, a white-on-white shirt, and a splash of yellow silk for a tie. The combination was nothing short of elegant, and yet he managed to look aggressively masculine. Exactly as he had looked last week in his jeans and cotton work shirt.

Continuing her survey, she eyed his stubborn jawline and determined chin. He had proved that he remained cool in an emergency. He would more than likely follow the path of logic, and be rational, reasonable and levelheaded. He would issue orders and expect them to be followed without question. Definitely a man to be avoided. Oh, sure, he was undoubtedly the answer to some maiden's prayers, but not hers. If she were going into battle, she'd want him on her side, but the last thing she needed was a man like that complicating her life.

Having reached that decision for the second time, she touched her napkin to her mouth and looked up as Dane spoke.

"You told me you were single. You didn't say if you were engaged or otherwise involved with a particular man."

"Is it important?" She grinned as she repeated the question he had asked earlier.

"Yes." His green eyes flashed silver as his smile slowly curved his mustache. His voice was soft, but perfectly audible, as he added, "I only go to bed with women in the first category."

Warily, she faced him across the width of the table. She spared a moment to remind herself ruefully that he was also the type to speak his mind. Too bad she hadn't thought of that sooner. She might have been able to divert him. Then, taking another glance at his calmly assessing expression, she decided it wouldn't have made any difference.

Carefully placing her napkin beside her plate, Kara

lifted her glass and downed the remainder of her wine in a couple of gulps. Fortified by a surge of warmth, she said, "This restaurant is wonderful, the meal was delicious, but your approach definitely needs a bit of polish. On a first date you should be subtle and charming. You definitely don't use the iron-fist-in-the-iron-glove method."

"But this isn't really a date. It was an emergency." At her skeptical look, he explained. "Two starving people were faced with a buffet. Drastic action had to be taken. Now, tomorrow," he continued, "will be another story."

She cleared her throat. "Tomorrow?"

He nodded. "Tomorrow will be an official date. I'll do my best to be charming. I should warn you, though, that I've never been big on subtlety."

"I could have guessed that," she murmured as he dropped several bills on the small tray that had accompanied the tab.

"I think we need to get a few things straightened out," she said as they strolled toward the parking lot.

"Where's your car?" he interrupted.

"At home. I went to the party with Judy. My partner," she said in response to his questioning look. "Look, about tomorrow—"

"Where do you live?" he asked, tucking her in the front seat and closing the door. Settling in behind the steering wheel, he turned and waited.

Kara briefly closed her eyes and sighed. Later, she decided. When he had taken her home and she had his undivided attention, they would talk. "Go back that way," she gestured. "Turn left at the light and go up the hill."

He swung into the stream of traffic and a few minutes later pulled up in front of an attractive complex of Town Homes. It resembled a vast Spanish hacienda, with whitewashed walls, red tile on the broken roofline, and an abundance of arches and decorative black wrought iron.

"Nice, isn't it?" Kara asked proudly.

"I've seen a couple of the units," was the noncommittal response.

"And?" When he hesitated, she said hastily, "Never mind. I don't think I want to know."

"They're well built for the price, and attractive. But the security is lousy. I could get in any one of them with a toothpick."

"Too bad they only issued us keys," she said coolly, releasing the seat belt and opening the door. "Think of the fun you could have had." His leisurely stride kept pace with her brisk steps down the center courtyard.

Relenting, she said, "Actually, you're right. The other night I had a housewarming party—I've only been here for a few weeks—and some of the guys said the same thing. So we tried an experiment. My girl friends and I locked the men out and secured the house. The object being, of course, to see if any of them could get in."

Her brows knitted in a scowl at the bland certainty in his voice. "How long did it take?"

"Only a few minutes. Five of them got in. Each a different way."

"That should give you some idea of how quickly a pro could do it."

"It did. You'll be happy to know that my security has been beefed up. We even formed a neighborhood watch system. Then I put new locks on the windows, dowels in the track of my sliding door and an alarm."

"What kind?"

"I don't know what it's called, but it seems to do everything but wash the dishes. It has water sprinklers—"

"To drown a burglar, I assume."

"And an alarm that's guaranteed to wake everyone in the complex," she finished, ignoring his dry comment. "As a matter of fact, a friend of mine was installing it when I left this evening."

"You didn't have a professional do it?"

"Oh, he's in the business," she said blithely. "Listen," she said, stopping near an octagonal fishpond, "you don't have to come all the way with me." After digging in her small evening bag, she pulled out her key and flourished it. "Thanks for dinner. It was really delicious." If she could pull this off, she wouldn't have to worry about a date, official or otherwise.

He snagged the key with one hand and turned her, cupping her elbow, with the other. "I can't resist a new gadget. I want to see your alarm. Besides, we haven't decided what time I should pick you up tomorrow."

She came to a stop in front of her door. "We're going to talk about that."

"Over a cup of coffee?" he asked hopefully as he inserted the key.

Kara had long been a devotee of British World War II movies. And for that reason, the sound erupting from her door was familiar. The ear-splitting wail of an air-raid siren rose in the darkness, shattering the peace of the courtyard. It was accompanied by a blinding strobe light and a stream of highly original curses from Dane. Windows flew open in the neighboring units, followed by the heads and shoulders of curious tenants.

"Turn it off!" Kara shrieked.

Dane glared first at her, then at the door. After a moment, he pulled the key from the lock. In the stunning silence that followed, they heard for the first time the shouts of various neighbors.

"Hey, Kara, that's some doorbell!"

"What do you do for an encore?"

"Want us to call the police?"

"Very funny," Kara responded, looking around the courtyard. "When I left, most of you guys were hanging over Terry's shoulder watching him install this thing. What happened?"

A deep, amused voice called down from a second-story window. "Terry had a little trouble with the wiring. He said he'd call you tomorrow."

"I thought you said your friend was in the business," Dane said grimly.

"He is," she insisted, looking up at him. "But he's new at it."

"How new?" he demanded, ignoring the amused comments floating down to them.

"I was his first customer," Kara admitted.

"Terrific." The disgusted word clearly indicated what he thought of her business arrangements. With calm authority, he turned to their fascinated audience. "We're going to try this again." His deep voice was clear in the still night air. "Once we're inside, we hope that you won't be disturbed anymore."

He turned, unbuttoned his jacket and handed it to Kara. Inserting the key, he winced as the keening wail resumed and the flashing light illuminated the two of them in a crazy-quilt pattern. Bundling her into the house, he pulled the key from the lock, bringing about instant silence, and slammed the door behind them.

"Where's the light switch?"

"Over here. Just a minute." She fumbled in the darkness, bumping into a chair that had strayed from its accustomed place, and said, "That's funny. It doesn't work."

"I'm not surprised. Your friend would be better off in another line of work," Dane said shortly. Sighing in exasperation, he asked, "Where's your circuit breaker?"

"My what?"

"The thing with switches that you fiddle with when the lights go out."

"I know what it is. You just surprised me. On the back porch."

"Do you have a flashlight handy?"

"No. But I have lots of candles," she offered.

"Fine. Anything." He turned, bumping into the wall, and heard something fall. A picture, he assumed. As a flicker of light grew to a small glow, he gave a grunt of satisfaction, then stared in disbelief as she handed him a tiny, feminine affair, roughly the size of a votive candle. "Sure you can spare it?" he asked politely.

"Patience is obviously another thing you're not big on," Kara observed sapiently. "If you'll just hang on for a minute, I've got a hurricane lamp over here."

Dane raised the candle above his head, glancing quickly at the layout of the room. His attention was momentarily drawn to a bright, woven wall hanging. He stood, candle aloft, trying to decide if his imagination was running away with him, or if he was staring at a cleverly crafted dragon. His decision was postponed indefinitely as a raucous, high-pitched whine invaded the room.

"What the—" The onset was so sudden and the sound so startling, that he whirled, snuffing the light, and Kara dropped the match she had poised to light the lamp.

"Now what have you done?" she asked, shouting over the din.

"I haven't done a damn thing," he said with asperity. "But in case you've ever wondered, your smoke alarm works just fine." He turned in the direction of her voice. "Can't you get that thing lit so I can shut off this hellish racket?" he demanded, raising his voice. Before the last word was out, she was pushing the lamp at him.

"No, you keep it. Hold it high enough so I can find the switch, but move back so you don't set it off again." He stretched, fiddled for a minute, and the nerve-racking whine stopped as if it had been sliced off with a sharp knife. They both exhaled in the sudden silence.

"Now, for God's sake, give me that thing," he said, reaching out a long arm. "I want to find the circuit breaker before the famous sprinkling system goes off."

Handing him the lamp, Kara listened as he strode through the kitchen and out the back door. He moved the same way he did everything else, she thought. With economy, precision and a certain masculine grace. The lights blinked on before she could pursue the thought.

His head cleared the doorway with an inch or two to spare as he came to stand beside her. He was dry, she noted. Obviously he had outrun the sprinklers.

"I'm afraid I knocked down your picture while we were groping around in the dark." His statement was matter-of-fact, not quite an apology. "If you'll get me a hammer, I'll put it back up."

Kara groaned inwardly. He was already convinced that she shouldn't be walking around without a leash. What she was about to say wouldn't help. "I don't have a hammer." She watched in fascination as a muscle in his jaw flexed.

He examined a series of pitted marks around the nail hole before turning to her. "Just how do you survive on a day-to-day basis?" he asked with genuine interest. "No flashlight. No hammer. Do you have any tools at all?"

She shook her head slowly from side to side, grinning at his disgust. "Not yet. But we've developed a system around here. There are men in this complex whose cooking would give a billy goat heartburn. There are some women who have been known to push a tack right through their fingernails. So we exchange talents. Home-cooked meals for hanging lamps, moving furniture, whatever. You should understand that. It's called reciprocity."

He frowned at the dented wall. "No man hung that picture."

"I did that one," she admitted.

"Well, get me whatever you used, and I'll put it back up."

She thought of protesting, then shrugged inwardly. Resting one hand on his arm, she bent over and removed one of her high-heeled sandals, and, straight-faced, handed it to him. He was quick, she had to give him that.

He looked from the spike heel to the wall. "Now I understand why it looks like you keep a tame wood-pecker around here. I'll put it up tomorrow." He crouched down, touched her ankle with warm fingers and slipped her shoe back on as she balanced herself with a hand on his broad shoulder.

Kara sighed at the expression on his face as he rose. Some men believed that she could be maneuvered into bed without a protest. Others expected a token argument and were mildly amused when they got it. They were not amused when they found themselves outside her door with only a swift good-night kiss for all their efforts. Whether or not the date was repeated depended upon how well they accepted the inevitable. Kara had companionship and affection to offer, nothing more. This man, she knew instinctively, wanted more.

Once or twice she had thought she might be in love, but she was not tempted to test the theory by leaping into bed. That leap had cost some of her friends far more than the loss of a night's sleep. Kara, always a quick learner, had so far delicately trod the tightrope of a busy social life while keeping the prowling wolves at bay.

Keeping this one at arm's length would be another matter if he decided that he wanted to be closer. He moved fast, and he was moving in her direction. Nor was he a boy to be distracted. As a matter of fact, she reflected, going off on a tangent, he didn't look like he had ever been a boy. Probably born with a scowl and knitted brows, a hammer in one hand and a flashlight in the other. She thought of her own helter-skelter family life, loving parents, a cluttered house warm with laughter, and decided that his discipline was unnatural. He needed humanizing, she told herself.

"What?" She was now seated next to him on the couch and had quite obviously missed something.

"I disconnected everything that idiot did in back. Did he remember to tell you that he'd have to chop holes in the walls and ceilings for the sprinkling system?"

Speechless, she shook her head. "I didn't think about that," she admitted.

"A couple of dead-bolt locks will keep this place safer than that birdbrained alarm. I'd advise you to call your friend and tell him the system is being returned and the home-cooked meal is canceled."

"Maybe he knows how to install locks," she countered.

"He's too late," Dane said flatly. "I'm here now."

"I promised him spareribs and all the trimmings."

"Tell him that the lady, *my* lady, has just gone out of the restaurant business."

Doing her best to ignore the possessive statement,

Kara commented idly, "I suppose you have a yen for something in particular. Pork chops? Prime rib? What's your weakness?"

"The only thing I crave right now is about five foot two, wrapped in a dress that looks like cotton candy."

"Sorry," she said lightly. "I'm never part of the deal."

His eyes narrowed in a silvery flash of satisfaction. "I thought so. This time, of course, it'll be different." He stretched his arm along the back of the sofa, enjoying her exasperated expression.

"There's no 'of course' about it," she snapped. Didn't the man ever listen? "But if you insist on playing handyman, bring on the locks, and I'll whip up a dinner. Whatever you want."

"I can cook or buy my own dinner. I'll take you," he said calmly.

"I'm not up for grabs," she informed him once again, speaking slowly, as if to someone who was mentally deficient. Turning to face him, she smoothed her dress over her knees and eyed him thoughtfully. "You really baffle me," she said finally. "Last week you couldn't wait to get rid of me, and tonight you're acting like I'm the only female left in San Diego County between eight and eighty."

"Last week I thought you were a teenager. Tonight I realized that you may be many things, but you're no kid." His look was as level as his voice. "I don't play out of my league."

"And I don't play at all," she informed him. "So I guess that takes care of that."

He stretched out comfortably, as if he were taking root. "About tomorrow. What time shall I be here?

How does a picnic sound? I'll need about an hour for the locks."

"Okay," she sighed. It had been a long day, and he had done nothing to make it an easy one. At the moment she wasn't equipped to deal with such bulldog persistence. "But somewhere between the locks and the picnic, I have to fit in a visit to Aunt Tillie."

"Fine," he said, rising abruptly. "I'll be here about eleven."

She picked up his jacket on the way to the door and held it out to him. "Oh! You never got your coffee. I'm sorry."

His gaze was enigmatic as he looked down at her. "After having three cups at the restaurant, anyone else would have recognized the request for exactly what it was: a delaying tactic. You're a bit gullible, aren't you?"

After a thoughtful moment, she nodded in agreement. "I guess I am," she said simply. "I trust people."

She opened the door and held out her hand. "Good night, Dane. Thanks again for the rescue. I'm sure my neighbors appreciate it, too." She was talking too fast, she knew, but the intent, silvery-green gaze on her face was unsettling.

He drew her to him and lowered his head.

She murmured something against his lips.

"What's the matter?"

"I've never been kissed by a mustache," Kara admitted with a grin.

"Well, if this is a first," he said, wrapping his arms around her slight form until she was wedged against his big body, "we'd better do it right. And in keeping with the good-neighbor policy, we'll be nice and quiet. No alarms or bells this time."

Several minutes later, Kara stared dazedly at the closed door. Quiet? The man was out of his mind. Her entire body was reacting just as idiotically as the front door had earlier in the evening.

Trailing through the house, turning off lights, she reached a firm decision. For the third time. She didn't need a powder keg like Dane Logan in her life. This time she really meant it.

Now all she had to do was convince him.

Chapter Three

Kara opened the blessedly quiet door the next morning at exactly eleven. She stepped aside as Dane came in. "Planning to rebuild from the ground up?" she asked, eyeing a tool box roughly the size of her coffee table.

"No. But I use more than a shoe heel and a nail file when I work." He gave her a long, appreciative look before he dropped the box at her feet and knelt by it. He was dressed casually in jeans and a green knit shirt. Curly dark brown hair poked out of the open neck and covered his muscular arms. He was even bigger than she remembered.

"You look like you're getting ready for surgery," she said, as he neatly laid out a drill, chisel and assortment of other tools. "Call me when you're through."

She walked to the kitchen, jeans-covered hips swaying pertly. A grin tilted his mustache as he watched.

"Do you want some coffee?" she asked, turning.

"Not now, thanks. Maybe when I'm done."

"What should I bring for the picnic? Somehow," she said, forcing a casual tone, "we never got around to talking about food last night."

"Nothing. My idea, my food."

"I won't argue about that. Next item," she said, as if checking off a list. "How much do I owe you for the locks?"

"Nothing." His tone was absent.

"Stop where you are," she commanded. Returning, she dropped down on the sofa and waited until he looked up at her. "That's not the way we do things here. I pay for anything that goes in my house. You do the labor for a meal, remember?"

"I told you last night that I don't want your food." His voice was level. "I was also pretty specific about what I do want."

"Then pack up your bag. No deal."

His hands didn't falter as he measured the door. "You need these locks. No strings attached this time. Compliments of the local handyman. Once I know you're safe, we'll settle the rest."

The silence stretched out. "At least tell me how much the locks cost."

He sighed in exasperation. "Fifteen dollars," he said, naming a fraction of the price.

Without a blink, she wrote a check and leaned over to lay it on the floor near the toolbox. Dane looked at the gleaming locks, the finest and most expensive on the market. Someday he'd have to visit her shop. It obviously wasn't a hardware store.

Two locks, more disconnected wiring and a hung picture later, they were in the big brown pickup, edging around Sunday tourists on La Jolla Boulevard. Kara gave directions automatically, her mind flying ahead to the small frame house that faced the ocean. Maybe her aunt would be wearing one of her less wildly exotic outfits, she thought optimistically. Acknowledging once again how fiercely protective she was, she leaned back and tried to relax.

Tillie was one of Kara's favorite people, but there was no doubt about it, she was different. She was small, wiry and spry. Her conversation, when it mattered most, was a disconnected series of starts, stops and unfinished sentences. What there was of it tended to be rambling and, to those who understood, filled with gentle warnings. The warnings resulted from what Kara's father irreverently referred to as "Tillie's trances."

Kara pressed her finger to a bell beside the freshly painted door. It was fire-engine red.

"Your aunt likes color," Dane observed, glancing around at hanging baskets of fuchsias and large pots of impatiens.

Kara nodded. "She changes the door to suit her mood. Give that thing a couple of whacks," she suggested, nodding at an imposing door knocker. It was a brass lion's head with a large ring in its open mouth.

Dane obligingly whacked and watched with resignation as a screw dropped to the ground and the ring stayed in his hand. The door flew open, and he looked down into the brightest blue eyes he had ever seen. Above them were peaked, silvery-gray brows and a mop of curly hair the same color, cut short in an optimistic attempt to subdue it. Below were firm, flushed cheeks that denied the years and a full mouth quirked with humor.

Kara performed introductions as he tried not to stare at the small woman's garb. She was swathed in something crocheted—possibly a tablecloth—that was secured at her tiny waist by means of a hot-pink cummerbund. Bright orange canvas espadrilles completed the outfit.

"You can call her 'Aunt' or 'Tillie,'" Kara concluded.

"Tillie," he decided, entranced, stretching out his hand to meet hers. "And I'm Dane."

"Of course you are," she assured him. As if, he thought, he had doubted the matter. "You're late," she continued cheerfully. "I expected you last week. No matter. Just close the door and we'll go out on the patio. Oh, dear," she said, noting that the door knob had now detached itself and was resting in Dane's palm. "Annoying, but not entirely unexpected. Just drop it over there."

Dane walked over to a large wicker basket festooned with a plaid ribbon. Gazing down, he realized that his booty would be joining a basketful of household items that, apparently, had already fallen off something else.

"It's all right," Tillie assured him. "That's what it's for. I just collect all the bits and pieces that come loose, and every few weeks Kara, or one of her friends comes by to reattach them."

Kara interpreted his raised-brow look correctly. "I'm not totally incompetent, you know."

"Then why is there always a full basket? You go ahead to the patio," he directed, "I'll take care of this." Turning, he fiddled with the knockerless door, opened it, and reappeared with his toolbox.

Ignoring the two women, who had dropped down into nearby chairs to watch, he replaced the knocker and knob on the door. "You'll have to show me where the rest of this stuff goes."

Tillie led the way at a trot. The dining room was the first stop. "The sconce goes there." She pointed to the wall, where a faint outline of the fixture could be seen against the painted surface. Patting Dane's arm in approval, she turned to Kara. "He's much nicer than the one with webbed feet."

Kara bit back a grin as he stiffened. He could think about that one for a while.

"I had a chat with Walter last night," Tillie said.

"Oh?"

"Have you had lunch?"

"Yes. What about Walter?"

"Would you like to stay for dinner?"

"Thanks, but no. What'd Walter have to say?"

"He said—would you like to spend the night?"

"Uncle Walter asked if I wanted to stay with him?"

"Of course not. *I* asked that. He just—is the traffic heavy today?"

"Not too bad for a Sunday," Kara answered patiently. "Is Walter worried about anything?"

"Which bathroom does this go in?" Dane held up a shiny faucet handle.

"This way." Tillie whisked down the hall, but before Kara could follow, Dane's arm barred the way.

"Webbed feet? Who were you dating, a duck?"

"I'll explain later. I promise. Right now, I have to pin Aunt Tillie down. Come on."

Dane bent over the sink, trying to make sense of the conversation. Interrogation was more appropriate, he decided after a moment.

The two women were perched on the edge of the bathtub. "Now," Kara said firmly. "Uncle Walter."

Tillie looked out the door and down the hall. "He just said it would be a shame to dent that nice brown truck. . . ."

Kara frowned at Dane as he jerked to attention.

"Exactly what is he upset about?" she prompted.

"There are always so many cars on Torrey Pines Road," she murmured. "There must be another way you could . . . If not, it won't be . . . There's no real . . . He said at the most it'll just be inconvenient."

At the end of two hours they had visited almost every room in the house as Dane nailed on something here and screwed back something there. Kara had given up all hope of eliciting a rational statement from her aunt. When they circled back to the front door, Tillie rested her hand on Dane's arm.

"Thank you. That basket's been full ever since I moved here. No, let's not say good-bye," she said, as Dane opened his mouth. "I'll see you again soon. Very soon. Don't wait for Kara to bring you back. You're welcome any time."

"This one is nice, but stubborn," she said, turning to her niece. "He won't be as easy to lose as the others."

Kara rolled her eyes imploringly to heaven, kissed her aunt on the cheek and waved as the truck moved slowly away from the curb.

"Now, about the duck." Dane's tone was uncompromising.

"A perfectly ordinary man," Kara protested with a gurgle of amusement. "No, not ordinary," she corrected herself. "Brilliant. A marine biologist from Scripps." She nodded in the direction of the famous institute of oceanography. "But Aunt Tillie took an instant dislike to him. We were going snorkeling one day; for some reason he tried on his flippers at her house, she saw him waddling down the walk and that was it. If, after your baptism today, you ever go back, you'll learn that she says exactly what appears in her mind. There's no winnowing process. I never took him back to see her."

"Good for Aunt Tillie! What about Walter? Who's he?"

"Aunt Tillie's husband."

"Where is he?"

"Dead. For the last ten years."

"I'm going to hate myself for asking," Dane said, "but how does she talk to him?"

"God only knows," Kara said literally.

"She really thinks she does?"

"So she says." If his brows lifted any higher, Kara noted, they'd slide into his hairline. "Do we have to go this way?" she asked as he turned onto Torrey Pines Road.

"It's the only way to get where we're going."

"Exactly where *are* we going?" she asked, momentarily distracted.

"My house. If you don't mind. A weekend picnic around here is like being in the middle of the zoo. I thought a barbecue would give us more privacy."

Exactly what we don't need, she thought, then shelved the topic for a more immediate one.

"I don't know if you made any sense of what Aunt Tillie was saying, if you were even listening, but Walter's warnings are not to be taken lightly."

"Were we being warned?" She wasn't surprised at the amusement in his voice.

"We were. And now we're on the street he said to avoid, in the nice brown truck that is, unfortunately, going to get dent—"

"Watch out!"

Dane's warning stopped her flow of words. The big truck barely moved under the assault of the red convertible. The thud and the grinding crunch sounded much worse than they actually were, she assured herself.

Dane was no longer amused. If his language was any indication, he was about to throttle a joy-riding teenager who had just lost control of his car.

"The damned idiot didn't even stop! He swung out of that side street without even looking! You okay?" At her nod, he ordered, "Stay here. I'll take care of it."

Ten minutes later he slammed the door and turned the key in the ignition. "Could be worse. At least he had insurance. Most of the damage was to his car. My fender's den—"

He almost choked on the word. "No," he said firmly. "It's a coincidence. That's all it could be."

Kara preserved a noncommittal silence.

"Damn it, I don't believe in psychics, clairvoyants or any other kind of so-called spiritualists. It's just not logical."

And that, thought Kara, was apparently that.

"Well? Aren't you going to say anything?"

"What can I say? All my life Aunt Tillie has known when things were going to happen. She hated to talk about it, but she'd practically lock me in the house when the forecast was gloom and doom. *If* it would happen was never debatable. The only real question was, would the occurrence be major or minor? Now she's got even that part down to a science."

He winced. "Please. Don't use that expression. Nothing could be less scientific. How did Walter get into the act?"

"When he died, he became a convenient scapegoat. Aunt Tillie no longer had the unpleasant task of convincing people that she had heard or seen something. She shifted all the blame to Walter. Now he's the bearer of all the bad news."

Dane snorted. There was no other word for it, Kara decided in amusement. It was definitely a snort.

"I suppose you'll tell me next that she consults a Ouija board when she's troubled."

"Never would I say such a thing." Her eyes darkened with humor. "There's no need. You see, when Uncle Walter isn't warning, he's advising."

"Oh, my God," he said in utter disgust as he turned into a long driveway.

"What are we doing here?" They had stopped at

one of the magnificent homes dotting the shoreline—or rather, the bluffs above it. "I'm not dressed to visit anyone."

"Who's visiting? I live here."

Who on earth was this man? Kara wondered. Dane Logan, he said. But who and what was Dane Logan? No ordinary contractor could afford this house. Not even an extraordinary one. In this area seaside property cost a fortune, and that was before an architect even came out to look at the site.

"Hey, wake up." He was at her side, opening the door and half lifting her out. "I'm ready for a swim. How about you?"

He swung open the ornamental wrought-iron gate, turned to the right and ushered her onto the patio. She barely took in the outsize pool, tables shielded by tilted umbrellas, brightly cushioned chairs and lounges, and a beautifully tiled deck, as he hustled her to a dressing room.

"You'll find something in here to fit. Help yourself. And don't take all day."

She looked around curiously as he disappeared. If he intended to keep her off balance, he was doing a terrific job. Though obviously, for him, it was normal procedure to toss out orders and walk away. Frowning, she reached for a white maillot that looked small enough. It was. It had the additional advantage of looking terrific, she decided, turning to glimpse her backside in the mirror. But he was going to have to find someone else to order about, she thought, turning to the door. A little of that went a long way.

He met her as she closed the door. "Good. You're ready."

He held out a hand, and she automatically placed hers in it. The top of her head just hit his collarbone, Kara noted. His skin was burnished to a deep tan, an all-over tan, she wagered mentally. She had the feeling that he spent a lot of time by the pool sans swim wear, that his brief, black suit was in deference to her presence. The dark, prickly hair that covered his arms was a furry mat on his chest. It tapered at his rib cage and stomach, and disappeared into the dark trunks. His long, muscular legs were liberally sprinkled with the same dark hair.

Enough, she told herself. He came on strong enough without any encouragement from her. It wasn't helping her cause to stand there goggling at him.

Tugging her closer, he draped an arm around her shoulders and steered her to the deep end. "You really are tiny, aren't you?" He hugged her lightly.

She shrugged. "Big enough for the important things in life. Besides, it's all relative. I don't feel small until someone like you towers over me."

He grinned and changed the subject. "How do you take your water? In inches, or one quick dive?"

Laughing, she admitted, "I've never done anything by inches. It's all or nothing."

They hit the water at the same time. Moving lazily at first, they broke into strong strokes, swimming laps. Heading for the side, Dane lifted himself effortlessly and leaned over to pull Kara up. She tumbled against his chest with a yelp, and he held her close until she wiggled in protest.

Dane slowly lowered Kara until her feet touched the deck; then, with an arm around her shoulders, he led her to a wide, cushioned lounge. Settling her on one side, he walked around and eased down on the other with a satisfied sigh.

"Let's soak up some sun, and then I'll feed you."

Kara stiffened when he stretched his brawny length next to her. Their water-cooled bodies warmed as they lay, touching from shoulders to toes.

"Relax," 'he advised blandly. "I don't ordinarily warn before I pounce, but I might make an exception in your case. Right now, sun's on the schedule. Next, food. Later, we'll see."

Closing her eyes on the thought that they would, indeed, see, Kara slept.

Later, after a shower and the promised steak dinner, Dane gave her a tour of the front part of the house. It had a comfortable elegance, she decided, enjoying the panoramic view of the Pacific from the living room. Wondering if he had designed, built and/or decorated it himself, she opened her mouth to ask.

"Sit down and tell me about your orphans," Dane suggested before she could draw a breath.

She dropped down on an ivory sofa, nodding as he offered her a cup of coffee. "Tell you what about them?"

"Everything. How you found them. What they're like. How your friends manage the whole thing."

"You've already made it clear that you don't sympathize with my project. Why do you want to know?"

"I told you. Last week I thought you were a kid telling me a crazy story. I want to see if it sounds any different now."

"Okay. But no nasty comments." She put down her cup and turned to face him. "About eight months ago I went to Tijuana because I'd heard of a man who was an artist with wrought iron. I'm always on the lookout for things like that for the shop. Judy handles most of the business, and I do the scouting for artwork. You should see some of the artisans I've found. They're unbelievable. Metalwork, stained glass, pottery—"

"The orphans," he reminded her.

"Oh. Well, anyway, I went down because Aunt Tillie wanted a wrought-iron stand for her plants. We couldn't find one the exact size, so we decided to have one custom-made. You might have noticed it on her patio. Up against the fence?"

"The orphans."

"So I decided if he did a good job on the plant stand, he just might be the answer to a little problem I was having at the shop. People were asking for customized ornamental wrought iron—everything from gates to bird cages—and I couldn't find anyone to—"

"The—"

"I know, orphans. Who's telling this, anyway? I'm getting to them. Juanito—he's called that because he's so big; actually, it means little John—works in the iron shop. He speaks English, and the old man, the artist, doesn't. I don't have an ear for languages and, all told, I know about thirteen words of Spanish. None of them were helping. He came over to untangle the verbal mess the old man and I were in."

She eyed Dane's bland face suspiciously. "Are you laughing at me? I know I take a long time to get to the point, but the background is important. Anyway, while I was telling Serefino, the old man, what I wanted, and Juanito was interpreting, and Serefino was saying he could do it, a toddler wandered in from the back room and started crying. I picked her up, asked who she belonged to, and Serefino started waving his arms and talking."

She fell silent, and Dane watched her expressive face as she seemed lost in the memory.

Shaking her head, Kara continued. "Juanito seemed reluctant to translate, but I eventually learned that he and his wife had taken in several abandoned children. The word had spread through town, and it wasn't uncommon to find a child left for him at the door of the shop. The little girl had been there when they arrived that morning.

"I asked Juanito how many they had, and he said eight. Naturally, I wondered how he managed to take care of them, because the money situation down there is so tight. We talked for a while, and when he saw that I was really interested, he invited me home to meet his wife. I went, I saw and I was conquered."

"Naturally," Dane said dryly.

"The walls of their little two-room shack were bulging. They said that their dream was to buy an abandoned farm several miles out of town. They could have a large garden, and room for all the children. It was going for five hundred dollars, but to them, it might as well have been five thousand. I thought about it for a while; then I remembered the day at Del Mar when I picked all the winners. I told them what had happened, and we decided to try our luck."

"Naturally."

"The following Saturday I met them at Caliente. It worked, and we left with enough cash to buy the farm and get things started. I go down as often as I can with clothes and things. Juanito and Carmella are hard-working and proud. They don't ask for help unless it's an emergency. So when they ask, I help."

"Naturally."

"You really are annoying, you know that?"

The telephone rang. Dane stretched an arm to the table beside him and punched a button on an ivory box. Tillie's voice flowed into the room.

"Dane, dear, I hope I'm not interrupting something important, but Walter didn't want you to worry."

"How did you find my number?" he asked, well aware that his name didn't appear in any telephone listing.

". . . I didn't know it was lost," she replied in confusion.

Kara giggled, muffling the sound with her hand when he scowled at her.

"What can I do for you, Tillie?"

"No, dear," she reminded him briskly, "I called you, remember? Because Walter didn't want you to worry."

"What am I not supposed to worry about?" he asked blankly.

"Has anyone else called you tonight?"

"No."

"Oh, good. Timing is still an uncertain element in these things. They will."

"Who will?"

"Walter never tells me everything. That's what's so annoying at times. But it's not as if a hiatus hernia is *terminal* or anything, is it? Well, now that I've told you, we'll all rest easier tonight. Good-bye."

"Wait a minute, Tillie. At least tell me this. How did you know my telephone number? I'm not listed in the book."

"I never use a book," she said in gentle surprise. "I just pick up the phone and dial. Good night."

The dial tone and Kara's smothered giggle were the only sounds in the room as he once again poked the button.

"Is that woman going to drive me crazy with mysterious messages every day?" he asked.

"Only when Walter tells her to."

"And now she's going to get a good night's sleep while I wonder what the hell she's talking about."

"But you don't believe in that stuff," Kara reminded him, "so there's no need to worry. Right?"

"You fight dirty, don't you?"

"Sometimes that's the only way for us midgets."

The telephone rang again, interrupting possible mayhem. This time, when Dane punched the button, a woman's tear-filled voice spoke.

"Dane?"

"Mom? What's the matter?"

"Oh, Dane. I've been so frightened. Your father's in the hospital."

"Where are you? I'll be right there." His voice was curt.

"Los Angeles. We're here for the Brattons' anniversary celebration, remember? But everything's all right now. I just didn't want you to hear anything that would worry you."

Dane felt the hair on the back of his neck lift. Kara sat quietly.

"What happened?"

"We're staying with the Brattons. After the party this afternoon we took a nap. Your father woke up in agony. We thought he was having a heart attack, so we called the paramedics." Her voice broke. "I've never seen him like that. He's always been so strong. He went into shock. It was awful. They rushed us to the hospital, and we've been waiting all this time."

"Why didn't you call? You know I would have come."

"I know you would. I didn't know what to do. But now I'm glad I waited. The doctor just came out and talked to us. It wasn't a heart attack or anything life-threatening. The shock was the most dangerous part. He said he'll release Dad tomorrow. What he has is a hiatus hernia."

Chapter Four

"Dane *Logan?* You're asking me who *Dane Logan* is?" Judy stared at Kara in disbelief across the width of the desk. They were sitting in the office at the rear of the shop. "You've been spending too much time with *los niños.*"

"The kids have nothing to do with it. Just tell me what you know about him."

"Let's put it this way. In a town that has millionaires crawling out of cupboards, he's still something special."

"How special?"

"Very. Cast your mind back about a year. Before you started playing games with the horses. Do you remember the articles in the paper about the big corporations that were leaving the large cities because of the traffic and smog? Or the article that told us that the companies were honoring our fair city by locating within its limits, bringing prosperity, more traffic and smog in their wake? Is it coming back now? Logan's conglomerate led the way.

"We now have Logan Computers being strung together in one part of town. Logan Condos and Town Houses are sprouting up in all directions. And the new hotel? Compliments of Logan architects, contractors and builders. You name it, Logan's doing it."

"You mean I had a multimillionaire hanging up my picture and screwing Aunt Tillie's tumbledown house together?"

"Did you really?" Amused blue eyes looked into dark ones. "How'd he take it?"

"Like every other man cadging a home-cooked meal. Willingly." She remembered quite clearly, however, that he had turned down the meal, and, even more clearly, his alternate suggestion.

"That's probably where he gets that I-have-spoken-now-hop-to-it! attitude," she mused aloud.

"What do you know about him?" Judy asked.

"Very little. He's perfected a technique called 'I ask, you answer.' And you know how I am. I talk in—"

"Paragraphs. What does he do?"

"Listens. Then utters syllables. Yes. No. The most I've gotten out of him is that he's thirty-three, a contractor, he thinks I'm a patsy, but all the same he wants—"

"What?" Judy pounced like a bright-eyed bird who had waited patiently for crumbs at a picnic. "He wants what?"

"Me." Kara admitted, cursing her loose tongue.

Why did her thoughts always emerge as words, tumbling out one after another, forming sentences beyond recall? Other people managed to remain silent with no trouble at all. Perhaps, she thought hopefully, some of Dane's clamlike ability would rub off on her. But, even if it did, it wouldn't help. Her face was as revealing as a road map. Never had she been able to run a convincing bluff. A lie was impossible. Apparently her thoughts were as clear as a ticker tape running across her forehead.

"I knew it!" Judy crowed. "The minute I saw him following you, I knew it."

"Well, you needn't sound so ecstatic. I like my life just the way it is, and that man is going to be nothing but trouble. He doesn't *listen*. He gives orders and assumes that I'll just fall right in with them." After a thoughtful silence, she brightened.

"I think, though, that my deliverance may be at hand. As you know, I introduced him to Aunt Tillie. He's already experienced Uncle Walter's benevolent mantle of protection."

"So soon?"

"Twice. Yesterday."

"Two in one day? That's coming on a little strong, isn't it?"

"He seemed to think so." Kara told her of the accident and the two evening calls. "He didn't have much to say when he took me home last night. Of course, that's not unusual. What I should have said is that he didn't leave me with any orders or directions for future meetings. He just saw me to the door, said good night and left. It's the most encouraging thing that's happened since—"

"Kara, can you come up front for a minute?" Beth sounded excited.

"What's the matter?"

"You won't believe it. You'd better come take a look."

Exchanging puzzled looks, the two women obeyed the summons. Standing beside Beth, they watched silently as a deliveryman, peering through the foliage and staggering beneath its weight, carefully lowered an enormous fern to the floor. He placed it beside three others that looked like clones. He turned and headed back to the floral van.

"Hey, wait a minute. Where're you going?" Kara asked.

He sighed. "There's still two more in the van. In another minute they'll be in here."

"But you're taking up all of our floor space. Put them back in the truck and take them away. We want fewer, not more."

"I can't, lady. They're paid for, and I was told to deliver them here. All of them."

"But—"

"Here's a card," Beth said, holding it up. "Maybe it'll explain."

With a sense of foreboding, Kara opened the envelope. Even though she had never seen the writing before, she recognized the bold scrawl immediately.

"What does he say?" Judy asked, never doubting where the gift had originated.

"He says Uncle Walter distracted him so much he forgot to tell me that he'd pick me up at seven tonight for—No! No more!" she called over the sea of green to the man, who was on his last trip. "Please, take them away."

His shrug was explicit. It informed her that he had done his job, crazy as it was, and now the ferns, and the problems, were hers. He returned to his van and drove away without a backward glance.

When Dane knocked on the door that evening, Kara yelled that it was open and to come in.

"I'm in here," she called. "You can't get lost, just keep coming."

He followed her voice down the entryway into the living room. "Why do you suppose I put those locks on your door?" he inquired.

"To lock burglars out when I'm not here," she answered promptly. "Certainly not to lock me in when I *am* here. Besides, it had to be you. It's neither six fifty-nine nor seven-oh-one, but exactly seven. Who else would it be?"

He changed the subject abruptly. "Is this something new in the way of meditation?"

"Don't be clever."

"Just checking. It's not every day that I find my hostess flat on the floor staring at the ceiling."

"Skylight," she corrected absently. "Not the ceiling. I'm watching to see how the evening light affects it."

"Why?"

"Because it's important. Also the morning and afternoon light."

"I'll bite again. Why?"

She sat up, holding her hands out to him. He obligingly pulled her up and waited.

"Because I want to make a stained-glass window for it, and the light pattern will affect the design and the colors I use."

"Have you ever made one before?"

She stared at his bland face, hearing, if it were possible, the raised eyebrows of disbelief in his voice.

"You should come down and see my workroom in the shop," she suggested dryly. "Yes, I've made one before. More than one. Many. And sold them. My only problem is, I don't know how to install it so it won't leak. A carpenter I'm not."

"But I am," he reminded her. "You make it watertight, and I'll install it the same way."

"It's a deal," she said, leading him into the kitchen and opening the refrigerator and waving a hand at its contents. "Name your poison."

"Beer. Very cold." He reached in over her shoulder, withdrew a can and pulled the tab while she poured herself a glass of white wine.

"Speaking of carpenters and such, why is it that you have so much spare time? I thought contractors spent part of the day sending workers out to locations and the rest of the day chasing them down and inspecting their work. Then at night—"

"Deciding where to send them again the next day? Wrong. Even so, I've done my share of whip-cracking today, and I rarely work nights. Which means we've got the rest of the evening to ourselves." He inspected her silky ice-blue caftan, which emphasized the silvery fairness of her hair. "That's nice, but you don't look ready to go out."

"Watch it," she warned. "Too much flattery completely unhinges me. But you do get points for being observant. This is not a going-out dress. The reason I'm wearing it is because I'm not going out."

She turned, pulled a plastic-wrapped salad bowl out of the refrigerator, peered in the oven for a satisfied moment and reached for some plates.

"I haven't thanked you for the clutch of trees you sent me this morning. They're lovely, but since I sold off the south forty, I had a little trouble deciding what to do with them. As they took up all the walking space in the shop, by unanimous decision they now line the sidewalk beneath our windows. It was also decided that since they were my gift, I got to move them and, in the future, water them."

She thumped the plates on the table and turned to look at him. "Have you ever heard of sending a single flower for a bud vase? Or a small bouquet? Have you ever heard the adage that says nice things come in small packages? Especially if the person on the receiving end owns a shop with very little extra space?"

He stood quietly, watching as she added dressing and tossed the salad. "And, if you're wondering, the reason I'm not going out is because of the way you *told* me we were. Your note, if I remember correctly, said 'Be ready at seven.' *Ordered* me to be ready at seven."

Throwing napkins next to the plates, she snapped, "I may be persuaded to do something. I may be motivated, enticed, convinced, lured or charmed, but I will not be—"

"Ordered. I'll try to remember that. What's for dinner?"

Her glare turned into a reluctant grin. "You're being difficult. I was ready for an argument. Fish. I'm not up to watching you devour another bleeding steak."

After they had eaten and cleaned up the kitchen, Kara led him back to the living room. She turned on the stereo and found a station with soft music while Dane looked around.

An interior decorator, he thought, would probably say that the room was a bold statement. Nothing at all like his cream walls and gold carpeting. The persimmon carpet and off-white walls were a perfect foil for the boldly striped couch of black, cocoa, persimmon and white. A scattering of chairs and cushions picked up the dominant colors for accent. The rest of the house reflected the same energy, with cheerful splashes of color. The result, he decided, was one of warm welcome.

He dropped down on the sofa and tugged gently on her hand. She settled beside him, and he draped an arm over her shoulders, pulling her close.

"This is nice," he commented lazily, turning his head to look down at her.

"Don't get too comfortable," she warned, trying—and failing—to edge away. "We're going to talk."

"Okay," he agreed amiably. "You first."

"Why didn't you tell me who you were?"

"I did. I told you my name. I couldn't have been clearer."

"You didn't tell me *what* you are."

"I said I was a contractor. And I am."

"You know what I mean."

"Yes." The word was grim. "I know. What do you want me to do? Wear a sign around my neck stating my credentials and net worth?"

"No. But I feel like such a fool. Because of your involvement with the city, I'll bet even the school kids know who you are. And what have I had you doing? Pulling wires, hanging pictures and propping up Aunt Tillie's house."

"In short, you've treated me exactly as you would any other man who can swing a hammer."

"Yes." She thought a moment. "But they understood and wanted it that way."

"So do I."

"That's not the point. I have the feeling you got conned into something you had no intention of doing."

His mustache twitched, and his smile was one of pure amusement. Green eyes gleamed beneath lazily lowered lashes. "Honey, do you honestly think you could make me do anything I didn't want to do?"

After thinking it over, she admitted, "Probably not."

"Definitely not. I'll let you know if I have any complaints."

He shifted, lifted her as if she weighed nothing at all, and settled her across his thighs.

She pressed her shoulders against the arm of the couch, found a comfortable spot for her head and looked up with a tolerant expression of inquiry in her large, dark eyes. "What's this all about?"

"You're too small," he complained. "I'm getting a crick in my neck trying to see you. And," he added after a moment, "I think I'm getting ready to pounce. I did tell you that I'd give warning," he reminded her.

"So you did. I don't think I've ever been officially pounced on before," she admitted with a grin. "What do we do now?"

"Whatever comes naturally. You join in whenever you're ready."

He moved again, lifting her higher. Her eyes closed as his lips touched her eyebrows. It wasn't, she reminded herself, as if she had never dated or kissed a man before. On the contrary. Being gregarious and, yes, popular, she had always had men around—friends, and those who wanted to be more. But now, for the first time, she realized that something had been lacking. Not in quantity, but quality. For the most part, the friends had remained. The others had drifted away, one disappearing as another appeared on the horizon.

But Dane, she remembered hazily, had announced his intentions. He wanted her in his bed. And not to sleep or, perchance, to dream. He wanted her awake and willing. And drifting away definitely wasn't part of his plan.

His hands brushed over her body, softly investigating this curve, that hollow. She murmured incoherently against his lips, and his arms tightened. At least her dress, the caftan, was relatively manproof, she thought dreamily. No back zippers, no front buttons. No encouragement there.

Doing what came naturally was potent stuff, Kara concluded a few minutes later. Not nearly as confident as she had been, she unwrapped her arms from around Dane's neck and tried to use them as a wedge. But a wedge, an effective one, required a certain amount of room. And there was none between his hard body and her soft one. None at all. Furthermore, both his large, warm hand and the hem of her caftan now rested on her bare thigh.

She pushed against his shoulders and slowly, reluctantly, he lifted his head. Dropping back against the arm of the couch, she drew in a deep, ragged breath. She was flushed and disheveled and looked, Dane thought, utterly delectable. And, he noted, her expression was no longer one of amused expectation.

It was the satisfied gleam in the silvery-green eyes that loosened Kara's tongue. "As the . . . pouncee in this affair, I request that we take a break."

Kara closed her eyes in exasperation as she heard her own husky, breathless voice. She took a peek at his expression and sighed. His eyes remained unwaveringly on her face. And even though he was leaning back, she could still feel the warmth of his arms, his lips, his—

She reined in her errant thoughts. That could only lead to trouble, big trouble, she decided. He was doing just fine on his own. He certainly didn't need her encouragement. She had the feeling, though, that regardless of what she did, he would stubbornly hack away at her objections until he got what he wanted.

Kara groaned silently. She was the peace-at-almost-any-price type and, whenever possible, avoided battles—of will, or any other kind. Up to now she had enjoyed her large circle of friends and changed partners so often that no relationship had ever gone beyond the platonic. She had seen too many friendships ruined by the onset of that old devil, sex. Charged atmospheres and frustrated passions were not for her. She *liked* her life the way it was. Simple. Spur of the moment parties; her orphans; laughter at the small absurdities of life. It was a *comfortable* life. She wanted it to stay that way. Was that asking too much?

One look at Dane's determined expression assured her that it was. He had the look of a man with a mission. And it didn't take a genius to figure out where he was directing his attention. He intended to shake up her life with the same casualness he would display when he shook sand out of a blanket after a beach party.

"Oh, my gosh!" She sat up and grabbed Dane's wrist, looking at his watch. "What time is it?"

"Almost nine-thirty. Why?"

"I'm late. I was supposed to make a phone call fifteen minutes ago." She slid off his lap, opened a drawer in a small desk and rummaged through it, sending a shower of paper to the floor. "I know I put it in here," she muttered. "It was on a blue piece of—here it is!"

"What's the hurry?" Dane asked.

"He doesn't have a phone, so he's waiting at a store," she answered absently as she checked the written number and poked buttons on the white receiver.

"Who?"

Kara mumbled in disgust as she hit the wrong button. "Will you wait a minute? Now I have to start all over." She tapped a nail impatiently as the phone buzzed in her ear.

"Juanito? Hi. I'm sorry I'm late. I . . . uh," she glanced obliquely at Dane, "got held up. No, no, everything's okay."

Her eyes remained on Dane's face, watching in fascination as his expression ranged from curiosity to recognition to grim determination. "I just wanted to make sure that the plans haven't changed for Saturday. About one?"

"No," Dane said, moving to her side. "Not at one, two, or any other time. You're not going."

"Just a minute," Kara said into the mouthpiece. "I can't hear you. There's some interference on this end." She glared upward. "You don't even know what I'm talking about, so will you please be quiet?"

"You're not going," he repeated calmly.

"For heaven's sake, it's just an innocent—What, Juanito? Oh. That may be a problem, but we'll work something out. Nothing is impossible, my friend."

"Some things are," Dane countered. "Such as your trip. There will be no trip." The words were spaced evenly for emphasis.

Kara's temper was normally slow to rise. Suddenly she knew why. Most of her life she had been surrounded by pleasant, tolerant, ordinary and *nice* people. Dane's arrival into her life had introduced her to a new species—determined, stubborn, provoking and *rude*. His interference in her affairs was awakening a dormant and unfamiliar side of her personality.

"You know something? You've known me for less than two weeks. And in that time you've decided that I'm a featherbrained idiot, and that I need a keeper. Well, I'm not, and I don't. I especially don't need you

frowning at everything I say and telling me what I can
or can't do. I told you earlier, I won't be—"

"Ordered. I remember. But someone has to—"

"No, they don't. But if they did, you wouldn't—"

"—and, apparently, I'm the only one with
enough—"

"—be the one I'd choose to—"

"—sense to see that you're heading straight for—"

"—help me cross the—"

"—trouble!"

"—street!"

Their words ended in a dead heat. Kara's exasperated tone all but drowned out Dane's level voice.

Suddenly aware of a crackling coming from the
telephone, Kara lifted the receiver to her ear. "What?
They want to close the store? Ask them to wait a
minute. I'm trying to get rid of the interference I told
you about."

Kara drew in a steadying breath and directed her
angry gaze back to Dane. "Good night," she said,
"and good-bye. I'll finish this conversation after you
leave."

Dane turned away and dropped back down on the
sofa. "You'll have a long wait," he warned, folding
his arms across his chest and settling down, Kara
thought in fury, for what looked like the rest of the
summer.

More agitated crackling prompted her to raise the
receiver once again. "I don't *know* how long," she
said, scowling at Dane. "As long as it takes."

They glared at each other, neither willing to back
down.

"If you think you're going down there without

me," he finally said through clenched teeth, "you're crazy!"

Not sure she had heard correctly, Kara stared. Recovering quickly, she asked, "In the truck?"

His nod was curt. "Why not? It's the closest thing I have to a tank."

"Juanito? Problem solved. See you at one on Saturday. 'Bye." After dropping the receiver in place, she turned to the simmering man.

"Why on earth you go on about these things, I'll never know. I'll be perfectly safe with—"

"How can you be safe with half the population chasing—"

"For heaven's sake! I thought I was the one who exaggerates around here. At the most, there were only five or six men. Anyway, that was then. It's not going to happen Saturday, because—"

"Damn right it won't, because I'll be there to keep an eye on you."

She rolled her eyes and asked the ceiling, "How did I ever survive all these years on my own?"

"That's what I've been wondering. Maybe Walter has been—"

"You leave my uncle out of this!" She dropped down in a chair across from him.

"I wish I could. What amazes me is that Tillie hasn't tuned into this whole thing."

"She knows all about it."

"Then why hasn't she tried to stop you?"

"Obviously because she doesn't see anything so bad about it. And what you expect to hap—"

"I'm sure that by now the word is out to watch for *la gringa rubia*."

"English, *por favor*."

"The blond American. Every two-bit hood at the racetrack will be looking for that head of hair."

"There's plenty of time to worry about that," she said carelessly.

"Five days isn't that far away."

"Your timing's off. We're not due to go to the racetrack for another two weeks."

She watched his changing expressions with fascination.

"Then will you tell me," he asked quietly, "just what the hell that telephone conversation was all about?"

"You mean, you thought—"

"I did."

"Well, it serves you right. It's a perfect illustration of what I've been talking about. You listen to a shred of information, weigh the paltry evidence, arrive at an erroneous conclusion and—"

"What was the problem he mentioned?"

"Transportation. But your truck took care of that."

"And the rest?" He eyed her widening smile with resignation.

"You've just insisted on supervising ten children at a beach party. They range in age from about one to fifteen, so they're a bit of a handful." She let that sink in before she softened the blow. "Of course, Juanito, Carmella and I will be there to help."

They regarded each other in silence. Dane's words, when they finally came, did not surprise her.

"I'm beginning to understand why you're still running free. There aren't many men who could—"

"Don't apologize for the poor quality of available

men," she said airily. "I fly free because I choose to."

He stood up, reached down and pulled her to her feet. "Little bird," he threatened softly, tucking her in the curve of his arm and directing her to the front door, "you're about to get your wings clipped."

"Resorting to threats so early in the game?"

He leaned back against the door, his green eyes taking in the amused anticipation on her face. He shook his head. "Promises. And you'll find that I take my promises very seriously."

Softly touching his thumb to her lower lip, he asked, "What time tomorrow?"

"Uh, no time," she replied after a moment, slowly turning her face away from the touch of his hand. "I'm teaching a weaving class tomorrow night. And Wednesday," she continued before he could ask, "I'm fixing Terry his spareribs. He deserves them, even if his work was all for naught. They'll help console him for having to return all that stuff. Thursday evening Judy and I have an appointment with our accountant. And Friday—"

"Is mine. I'll be here at seven."

She eyed him stonily. "Have I ever told you just how much I enjoy being bossed around?"

"No." He grinned suddenly. "It's probably the only thing you haven't told me. But I'll give you all the time you want on Friday." Drawing her to him, he lowered his head. His lips brushed hers, strayed to an elusive dimple in her cheek and returned.

Minutes later, the door closed softly behind him. Kara sagged against it, then jumped as he reminded her, "Lock the dead bolt. Now."

Orders again, she thought in irritation. The feeling intensified as she became aware of her ragged breathing, loud in the silent room.

As he drove home, Dane's thoughts returned to the cheerful apartment. He still had the taste of Kara on his lips and the feel of her slight body against his. Friday. A long time to wait to hold an aggravating, captivating, maddening and enchanting woman in his arms. Of course, once she was his, she would settle down. She would understand that she couldn't run around risking life and limb, lopping off chunks of a man's remaining years with her hair-raising antics. Of course she would.

Chapter Five

Dane turned the pickup through the entrance in the white adobe fence, drove slowly across the dirt yard and stopped in the shade of a scrub oak. The children, alerted by the sound of an unfamiliar vehicle, instinctively edged closer to each other. Then, recognizing Kara's silvery head, they swarmed around the truck like hummingbirds at a blossoming plant.

"Cariña! Cariña!"

"What are they saying?" Dane asked, puzzled. Before Kara could reply, he recognized the word.

"They've never quite figured out my name," Kara said. "That's what they call me." She opened the door and slid to the ground.

Dane got out slowly on his side, watching as the children pressed close to her, clamoring for a hug, a kiss, a special touch. *Cariña,* a variation of their word for love, affection. She had been well named.

He turned his attention to the building before him. It was an adobe, thick walled and newly whitewashed. A large vegetable garden stood off to one side and extended behind the house. The area in front was dirt, carefully raked and very tidy. Everything, he noted, was as neat as the proverbial pin. As he turned to take in the rest of the grounds, Kara approached with the children and two adults in tow.

"Dane, I want you to meet Carmella, Juanito and the rest of the crew."

He looked at a large man with a neatly trimmed beard and steady eyes. A pretty, plump woman stood quietly beside him. After a moment of mutual regard, the three smiled and shook hands all around. Kara released a small sigh of relief.

"This part," she said with a smile, "requires some concentration." She brought each of the older children forward, one at a time. Emulating the adults, they stepped forward and gravely shook hands. "This is Ruben, Benito, Carmen, María, Oscar, Alberto and Elena. And these munchkins are Juanita, Stella, Alonzo, Eduardo and Elva." Dane squatted down to be at eye level with the tots and, to his surprise, all but the smallest darted or staggered over, then reached up to hug him. The baby, still in Kara's arms, flirted with him, then buried her face in the curve of Kara's neck.

"You've now been hugged and stamped with approval. Would you like a tour of the place?"

"Yes. I thought you said there were ten."

"The family has grown in the last few days. Let's go this way," she said, following Juanito and Carmella.

"You should have seen this place when they bought

it. It was a mess. I brought some of my hardier friends down for a weekend. We camped here and created miracles. And, of course, Juanito always works like a man possessed."

Dane was shown through the girls' and boys' dormitories, Spartanly furnished with bunk beds and threadbare blankets. The cement floors were bare, but spotless, and there was a stall shower at the end of each room. The dining room had two long tables with benches and several high chairs for the toddlers. A massive gas stove stood against one wall of the kitchen. Open shelves were filled with loaves of bread and canned goods. The rest of the rooms were much the same: bare walls, cement floors and little furniture. By rights, Dane thought, it should have been dismal and depressing. But it wasn't.

Carmella's optimism, Juanito's determination, the happy chatter of the children—not to mention Kara's eagerness to spread largess from the racetrack, he decided wryly—made the rooms ring with laughter, contentment and hope.

Having shown off everything they possessed, the children began milling anxiously. "Trot out your Spanish," Kara directed Dane, "and assure them that we'll head for the beach in a few minutes. We just have to arrange the logistics."

Everyone agreed that the children would be safer in Dane's high-sided truck. Within minutes, a large chest filled with iced drinks and boxes of food were transferred to Juanito's flatbed truck with homemade wooden sides. Carmella and Kara each held a toddler.

"Okay." Kara grinned up at Dane. "We're ready. Tell the big ones that they're responsible for the little ones, and if even one of them stands up or hangs over the side, we stop and come right back."

Before Dane had finished, kids of all sizes were crawling into the bed of his truck. The ones who couldn't make it on their own were handed in. The tailgate was secured and, within minutes, the two trucks were on the road.

"If you can't speak the language," Dane asked with interest, "how do you communicate with the kids?"

"Slowly, and with lots of body language. They don't seem very interested in the few words I know. Can't say that I blame them. The sum total of my knowledge is just about exhausted when I explain to out-of-state tourists that in Spanish a *j* is an *h*, and two *l*s are a *y*, which, of course, is why La Jolla is pronounced *La Hoya.*"

"Have you ever considered taking a Spanish class?"

"Of course!" she replied in amazement. "I *have* taken them. Again and again. But nothing makes sense or sticks with me. Everything sounds the same. In class exercises someone would ask me how I felt and I'd tell them my name. Or they'd ask my name and I'd say I was fine. The kids point me out as the crazy lady who went to the store for eggs and asked for a dozen Thursdays." She grinned at his sudden crack of laughter.

"Admittedly, the words *huevos* and *jueves* look different on paper, but when I say them, they come out the same. I also made the mistake of memorizing a few questions to use in the shop with Spanish-speaking customers. Things like 'May I help you?' and 'Is there something in particular you would like to see?'"

"Why was that a mistake?"

Kara shifted Elva to her other shoulder and said simply, "Because they answered me. They were so delighted to hear something familiar, torrents of words poured out of them. They never stopped, even to breathe. They would call in their sisters and brothers and aunts and uncles who were waiting outside, and *they* would talk to me."

She looked up at him. "What I should have learned to say was, 'Stop! I only know how to count from one to ten,' or, 'You're not using any of the thirteen words I know. It wasn't funny at the time," she said, grinning despite herself. "Now, I point and raise a questioning eyebrow. If that doesn't work, we play charades. We have a good time, and no one seems to mind."

No, he thought, keeping close to the truck ahead of him and automatically coping with the heavier traffic, they wouldn't mind. He wasn't the only one drawn to her spontaneity and warmth. He wasn't the only one who watched for the smile that began in her eyes, curved her lips then illuminated her entire face. She attracted people to her with the same ease that a magnet drew metal filings.

His hands tightened on the steering wheel. How many men had seen themselves reflected in her dark eyes as they bent to kiss her? How many had laced their fingers in her silvery hair and tugged her closer? How many had lain beside her in a bed warm from their naked bodies and stroked her breasts, listened to her soft cries? How many had—

"Dane? Hey, what's the matter? You look awfully grim for someone who's going to a beach party."

He shook his head, replying absently as he looked into her upturned eyes. Eyes fringed by absurdly long, dark lashes, eyes that shone with concern and . . . and what? Friendly acceptance? He didn't know what her eyes held, but he realized with a surge of exultation what they didn't hold. They lacked that gleam of unconscious sensuality, the look of knowledge, of experience. By God, he thought triumphantly, if there had been *any*, there hadn't been many. And now he was here. It's as simple as that, he thought. He was here. There would no longer be *men* in her life. Only a man. Only him.

Kara cuddled the baby, talking soft nonsense to her, unaware that her fate was being decided by the man beside her.

The afternoon passed in flurry of chaotic activity. The boys pulled an old blanket out of the truck, dumped firewood in it and, each hanging on to a corner, hauled it to an area away from the crowd. Answering Dane's questioning look, Kara explained. "We make a point of staying to ourselves because there are so many of us. It's easier to count heads every few minutes."

A soccer game was begun, but it soon turned into a jumbled version of boys-versus-girls touch football, with Dane the coach and captain of one team. Kara was called in to serve as the other captain when Juanito decided he wanted to referee.

"You don't even know how to play," Kara objected. "How can you call a foul?"

"I'll tell him when," Dane said with a straight face.

"Have you ever heard of a conflict of interest?" Kara inquired.

"What's the matter, tough stuff, afraid of the competition?"

"How can you even ask?" she wondered aloud. "I have a team I can't talk to, a rigged referee, and my opponent was probably a college all-star. That just makes it interesting." She turned away from Dane's lazy grin and motioned her team into a huddle.

The first play set the tone for the rest of the game. Her girls treated the ball like a hot potato and finally tossed it to Kara. She yelped and started running. Evading Dane's boys was the easy part. Clutching the ball, she looked around and saw Dane loping at an angle to intercept her. His expectant look filled her with determination. She decided she would make a touchdown or die in the attempt. At the same time, she wondered if she had retained any of the speed she had developed from her sprinting days in college.

Fairly flying over the sand, she heard the kids screeching behind her and, sooner than she'd thought possible, the thud of Dane's feet. Just as she thought she had made it, she was tackled and gently tumbled to the sand. When she stopped rolling, she was flat on her back, wrapped in Dane's arms, protected from the impact by his big body.

She looked up at him as his hands slid down and rested on her rounded bottom. Her glance rose a notch and she found herself staring at a circle of brown, grinning faces. Drawing in a deep breath, she yelled, "Foul! Referee, call a foul! We're playing touch," she muttered to Dane, "not tackle. Remember?"

"I'm touching," he said softly, tightening his grip. "Believe me, I'm touching."

"Where's the referee?" Kara called as she tried to wiggle out of Dane's embrace and immediately discovered that she was locked in place by his arms. The circle of faces parted, and she discovered Juanito with his back turned, intently watching a sea gull.

"Some help he is," she muttered.

Dane leaned down, brushing his lips against hers. "He can't help you. No one can. This is just between us."

Kara had a sinking feeling that he wasn't talking about a football game. Ignoring the implication of his words, she prodded his shoulders. "Okay," she agreed briskly, "I'm beyond help. But, *you,* coach, have a problem. You've set a terrific example for these grinning little wretches. They're going to try tackling each other, and we'll have an epidemic of broken bones. Before they get any ideas, you get on your feet and talk to them. Tell them you fell on me, tell them anything, but make sure they don't try it."

Dane sighed, reluctantly shifted his weight and stood up. Reaching down, he grasped Kara's hand and effortlessly pulled her upright. He gently smoothed a lock of hair behind her ear before turning away.

Kara watched as he squatted down and signaled for attention. He was gesturing and talking earnestly as she walked over to Carmella.

"Your man, he is *muy guapo,*" Carmella said softly.

"Handsome is as handsome does," Kara answered. "Besides, he's not mine."

Carmella arched a disbelieving eyebrow that spoke volumes.

Kara was called back to the game before the

interesting conversation could be developed. Whatever Dane had said was effective, she noted, because the game proceeded without even the most adventurous attempting a tackle.

The rest of the afternoon spun itself away as everyone headed for the water. The older children were sorted out by swimming ability and supervised by the men. Juanito worked with the nonswimmers, and Dane taught the others the trick to body surfing.

Kara and Carmella watched as the little ones staggered to the water's edge, squealed as waves lapped at their ankles and either plopped down in an inch of water or danced away as fast as their chubby legs would carry them.

Mealtime was a boisterous, messy affair. Wire coat hangers were carefully straightened out; then wieners were skewered on them and roasted over the bonfire. The bobbing pieces of meat, ranging from raw to charred, were slapped between buns and slathered with mustard, catsup and salsa.

"I don't know how you do it every day," Kara said later to Carmella. Hunger had been temporarily assuaged, and the firelight was reflected on a circle of young, contented faces.

"God provides the time and energy," the other woman said serenely.

The moon was hanging high in the sky, casting its silvery glow over the water. The gentle waves broke softly on the sand and, for a moment, all that was heard was the crackling of the fire and the distant sound of mariachis, musicians strolling from one group to another, singing and playing guitars.

Ruben lay back, cupping his head in his hands,

looking at the sky. Suddenly he nudged Alberto, pointed up and said something. Alberto looked, poked Carmen and repeated the words. Soon all of them were staring at the sky. They turned to Kara, chattering among themselves, and nodded in satisfaction.

"La señorita como la luz de la luna," they agreed.

Kara turned puzzled eyes to Juanito. Amusement lit his eyes as he explained. "They say your hair is the color of the moon. They have decided that tonight you are the lady of the moonlight."

"La señorita como la luz de la luna," they said once more in satisfaction.

"No, *chicos,*" Dane said firmly. *"Mi señorita."*

Even Kara recognized the stressed possessive word. Not *the* lady, but *my* lady. She turned dark, indignant eyes on him. But the hot words on her lips were stopped when he smiled, wrapped his arm around her waist and pulled her close to him.

Juanito's eyes met those of his wife, and he nodded. Turning, he reached for his guitar and began strumming softly. Carmella sang, nodding for the others to join her.

"Born diplomats," Dane murmured in Kara's ear as his arm tightened.

Kara felt him wince as her elbow dug into his ribs. "You're pushing, Logan," she whispered. "You'll get yours later."

"I can hardly wait."

Before long, the music lulled the babies to sleep. Carmella looked around and said with a smile, "We should go before we have twelve sleeping *niños* on our hands."

Yawning youngsters reluctantly piled into Dane's truck and were covered with blankets. Before the men had packed the supplies into the other truck, the children were asleep. When they reached the farm, the older ones were awakened and they groggily stumbled to their beds. The babies were tucked in without being disturbed.

Kara hugged Carmella and Juanito. "Good night. It was fun. We'll try it again soon."

The couple turned to Dane. "Come back and see us. Any time."

"Thanks, I'll do that." He nudged Kara toward the truck. As they drove out of the yard, they called one last good night and turned onto the road.

Kara's sigh combined fatigue and contentment. Dane draped an arm around her shoulders and urged her closer. They were silent as they passed the huge, paved parking lots of the racetrack, rode through town and passed the Customs area.

Dane looked down at the windblown, silvery hair. "Why so quiet?"

Kara stirred, wondering how she had ended up pressed against him from shoulder to knee. "Partly tired, partly thinking about Benito. There's something about him that bothers me, and I can't put my finger on it."

He dropped a hand on her thigh, gently kneading. "Think out loud. Maybe between us we can piece it together."

"It's something about the way he moves. I was watching him play ball this afternoon. His coordination is off, his . . . responses are too slow. It worries me. I hope he doesn't have some awful degenerative disease."

"You're right," Dane said thoughtfully. "I didn't notice it while we were playing, but now that you mention it, I think there is something. I doubt that it's serious, though. When I was about his age, the kid next door to me was like that. Always getting zapped with baseballs, never able to catch a football. We thought he was just a klutz."

"What was it?"

Dane grinned. "He needed glasses. He never said anything because he thought everyone saw things fuzzy the way he did."

"Glasses!" Kara burst out in relief. "I never thought of that. I'll mention it the next time I see Carmella." She fell silent again, mentally adding the price of glasses to the cost of clothing for the two latest additions to the rapidly growing family.

"Now what?" Dane asked in resignation.

"Nothing. Well, almost nothing. No, nothing," she said decisively, remembering his unequivocal speech about helping people at their first meeting. He might have softened enough to help supervise a beach party, but she wasn't going to supply him with the material for another "patsy" lecture.

She was still brooding as she handed over her keys and watched him open her front door.

"I'd give a lot for a cup of coffee right now."

Kara eyed Dane suspiciously, remembering the last time he had invited himself in voicing the same desire.

"I mean it this time," he assured her as he strode toward the kitchen. "No instant or decaffeninated, though. It's been almost twelve hours since I've had any, and I want the real stuff, brewed. Do you have the makings?"

"Of course I do, but I don't especially want to make it," she said, wondering why this man always brought out the worst in her. Maybe, she decided, it was because tact never seemed to work. It took a bulldozer to make a dent in his hide. "In case you haven't noticed, I'm dirty and tired. I want to take a shower and go to bed."

She tried leading him to the front door and lost him at the dining-room table.

"What's this?" he asked, looking down at a jumble of photos spread all over the table.

Leaving the door with a reluctance he ignored, she came to a halt next to him. "My mother gave me a box full of old family photos. I'm trying to organize them chronologically; then I'll put them in an album."

"My God," he said suddenly, seeming to take in her appearance for the first time. "You do look like you've been through the wars." He turned her around and gave her a gentle shove. "I'll make the coffee while you shower; then we can look at your pictures."

"You don't want to do that," she protested. "There's nothing worse than looking at pictures of people you've never met." She stopped for the simple reason that he was no longer there. Listening to the noises coming from the kitchen, she finally shrugged and headed for the shower.

She was right, of course. Nothing put him to sleep faster than someone reaching for a family photo album. But for the first time in his life he was intensely curious about a woman. He wanted to know everything about her. Was her hair that silvery shade when she was a child? Did she like bananas, ever wear braces? Was she accident-prone? Did she always have a penchant for the underdog? How old was she when she started dating? Had her smile always been so blinding? What was her favorite color, flavor of ice cream, sport? Did she cry at sad movies?

Of course she did, he decided, pulling down coffee mugs. She probably also cried at those with moments of triumph or tenderness, or happy endings. While waiting for the coffee, he found the cream and lifted the lids of various containers. The last one yielded what looked like homemade chocolate chip cookies. He filled a small bowl with a handful and took everything to the cluttered table.

Kara reluctantly passed over a blue knee-length robe and reached for a clean pair of jeans and a cotton shirt. After dressing quickly and brushing back her towel-dried hair, she frowned into the mirror. She wasn't about to put makeup on this late in the evening. He'd just have to take her as she was. No, scratch that, she advised herself hurriedly. Too frequently for her peace of mind he had the look of a man who intended to do just that.

She found him examining stacks of photos with absorbed interest. He had made himself very much at home, she noted absently. The cookies were almost gone, and his cup looked ready for a refill.

"Fascinating, aren't they?" she asked, watching him as he kept the pictures in their original order by placing them facedown in a pile. He swept them up and carefully returned them to their assigned space.

"Um-hmm." He slid her mug closer to him and

eased his chair back a bit. "Sit here," he directed, sliding his arm around her waist and easing her down on his thigh.

"I'm too heavy," she objected as she perched gingerly on a leg so muscular it felt like a wooden beam.

"I can handle it," he assured her. "You may eat like a lumberjack, but you still don't weigh any more than a butterfly. Come on, I want you close so you can tell me who these people are. Is the coffee too potent?"

As she obediently lifted her cup to test the strength, Kara realized that once again she had been outmaneuvered. Slick technique, she decided. Every time she argued about something, he gave a rational explanation and asked a question that changed the subject. Not bad. In fact, it was well worth cultivating.

For the next thirty minutes she pointed out friends and relatives and answered questions. Yes, she was allergic to animal hair, but that didn't stop her from bringing home stray dogs. Yes, that was her at fourteen wearing a ponytail and flashing braces. There she was learning to water-ski. Not exactly star material, but she finally managed to stay up on her feet.

Kara eventually set her mug down with a definite clink. "You've seen my father, my mother, two brothers and assorted branches of the family tree. You even got a glimpse of Uncle Walter, for heaven's sake. That's enough, the end, finis."

She raised her hand to cover a huge yawn and stood up. He rose with her, and she mumbled, "You make wonderful coffee, but even that can't keep me awake. You're going out the door. I'm going to lock that nice, shiny dead bolt and fall into bed."

As she turned to follow her own excellent advice, she found that her body wouldn't cooperate.

Dane was perched on the edge of the table, legs slightly apart. Kara was pressed against him, fitted to the lean length of his body as if tailor-made. His grasp was light, but she knew she wasn't going anywhere until he let her. The silvery flash in his eyes alerted her drowsy senses.

She opened her mouth to protest . . . and knew she was too late. His breath was warm on her face. Even as she tasted the coffee on his lips, she stretched and slipped her arms around his neck. Dane's hands slid down into her back pockets and pressed her close against the undeniable evidence that his attention had not been entirely on photographs.

Kissing Dane, she thought dazedly, was a bit like going under an anesthetic. It would be so easy to give up, to let him take control. The idea was tempting, and for a moment she did nothing but lean against him and savor the touch of his lips, the warmth of his body.

"Dane?" The whisper was a puff of sound against his mouth.

"Hmm?" he murmured without moving.

Slowly, reluctantly, her hands slid to his chest. She was momentarily distracted as she felt the crisp hair beneath his thin shirt. Her fingers lingered, then curled into small fists and tentatively pushed.

"Hmm?" he repeated, raising his head a fraction of an inch.

"We'd better stop right now, or God only knows where we'll end up," she said shakily.

"We both know where we're going to end up. In my bed."

"Maybe," she said, getting her second wind.

"No maybe about it," he said flatly.

"But not tonight," she persevered.

"No, not tonight. When it happens, you won't be dead on your feet."

"In that case, may I have my pockets back?" she asked with a straight face.

Tightening his hands again around the softly curved flesh, he pulled Kara against him and leaned down for one last, hard kiss. Raising his head, he stared at her with narrowed eyes, then turned them both toward the door.

Feeling as if she had had a narrow escape, Kara silently released a sigh of relief. Lowering her lashes, she meekly agreed to lock and bolt the door.

"I'll be by about one tomorrow," he said, still in the doorway.

"Where are we going?" She was definitely going to have to teach him how to ask. His orders were beginning to get on her nerves.

"Del Mar."

"A racetrack? That's like taking a busman's holiday," she protested. "I don't have any fun at the races."

"I have an overwhelming desire to see a semi-psychic in action," he admitted. "Just once. I'll never ask you again."

"All right," she capitulated slowly, suddenly remembering Benito's glasses and the additional clothes. "But you have to let me do it my way. You're not to try to convince me that your system is better and pressure me to change my mind."

"Would I do such a thing?" he asked innocently.

"You would. You do. Constantly."

"I'll have to work on that, won't I?"

"You certainly will," she murmured as she locked the door and turned out the lights. "You certainly will."

Chapter Six

"I am absolutely, positively not superstitious," Kara muttered aloud as she smoothed down the lavender sundress and sprayed on cologne. Dane was due in ten minutes. Ten minutes—just long enough to drive herself crazy. Just because it had been her policy to have other people bring the money and do the betting, it didn't mean it wouldn't work if she supplied the cash, did it? Of course it didn't. Surely a simple change in procedure wouldn't affect her ability to pick the winners. She knocked on wood and crossed her fingers.

The cause was still the same, the children still the beneficiaries, she reasoned. It would make no difference at all that her dollar bills would be slid across the counter instead of Juanito's pesos. If this peculiar ability to pick a winner was God-given, as Aunt Tillie maintained, would He abruptly withdraw it just because she was trying to prove a point?

She wished that her intentions were as straightforward as they ordinarily were. This time, unfortunately, there was a bit of ego involved. Plus, she reluctantly admitted, a desire to beat Dane's systematic approach to smithereens. Just once, she would like to knock him off his patronizing perch, to dent his belief that whatever she did, he could do better. No, she admitted, as a brisk rap sounded on the door, her motives were far from pure.

An hour later, sitting in a shaded area of the racetrack on the outskirts of San Diego, she sighed in relief. She had opened the program, afraid to look at the names of the horses in the first race. But there they were. Almost as if someone had taken a felt-tipped pen and highlighted them.

Dane's eyes had a quizzical gleam. "Who do you like?"

"Banjo Eyes," she said firmly.

"You've got to be kidding," he said in astonishment. "That's a dog, not a horse. She hasn't been among the first five in her last ten races."

"I don't care if she's tottering out of her stall with an impacted wisdom tooth. She's the one."

Dane stood up to go place the bets. "To show?" he asked hopefully as he took her five dollars.

"No, she's not coming in third. Bet her to win."

Kara could see by the set of his shoulders that Dane thought she was crazy. He was probably also wondering how on earth the children had a roof over their heads if they were dependent upon her winnings.

Ten minutes later, she was vindicated. Dane had all but pulled his horse around the track with body language and hoarse shouts, and still it had come in fourth.

"I don't believe it." He looked at her accusingly, as if she had used black magic. "That horse of yours ran the fastest race of her career. How do you account for that?"

"I can't," she said simply. "I don't even try. I just tell people how to bet and watch them collect their money."

"Do you know what the odds were?"

Kara sighed. "No. But I'm sure that you do."

"Twenty to one."

Her brows knit as she thought about that, and Dane's exasperation grew. "I won a hundred dollars," she announced in a pleased tone.

"And I lost two."

"Dollars?"

"Hundred."

"Dane! You shouldn't bet that kind of money! Especially when you're going to lo—" Swallowing her impetuous words, she bent over and looked intently at the program. Her head immediately bobbed up. "Oh, gosh, I suppose I should pick up my money."

"I'll do that when I place your next bet." He eyed her curiously. "What's your choice for the second race?"

"Bojo's Boy. Put my hundred on him to win."

He looked appalled. "No! Damn it, Kara, he's a mudder. He likes a wet track, and it hasn't rained in months."

"Well, he's just going to have to learn not to be so picky. He'll run on a dry track and like it."

"You're really serious, aren't you?" Frustration had deepened the green of his eyes.

She couldn't help it; she laughed up at him. "Put your money on him, Dane. He's going to win."

"No way. Your method is as haphazard as drawing a name out of a hat. You were lucky the first time, but this one's not coming through for you. I'll bet on one that at least has a chance."

Fifteen minutes later, Dane stoically tore up his tickets. He scowled at Kara. "You now have seven hundred dollars."

"How much did you lose?"

"Never mind."

"This time," she said, "I want you to keep six hundred for me and bet the rest on Harpsichord."

"If you're so sure of yourself, why not bet the whole thing?"

"I try to keep a low profile, not to make any bets big enough to attract a lot of attention."

"Too bad you didn't think of that the last time you were in Tijuana. You wouldn't have—did you say *Harpsichord?*" His voice rose in disbelief.

She nodded.

"Kara," he lowered his voice to somewhere near its normal tone, "this time you're dead wrong. I'm telling you, don't waste your money. This is a high-strung horse, and only one jockey has ever ridden him. The jockey broke his arm last week. I don't know why they didn't withdraw him."

"The jockey?" she asked in bewilderment.

"The horse." His tone was that of a man pushed beyond his limits but still trying to be reasonable. "He'll fight this new jockey every step of the way. Pick another one," he urged.

Kara looked at the program again. "No," she said definitely. "It's Harpsichord."

Dane turned to face her. His hand was warm on her arm, his voice filled with utter exasperation. "Why the hell can't you listen to reason? I'm only trying to help you."

She patted his hand. "I know you are, and I appreciate it. But don't you understand? This has nothing to do with logic or common sense."

Her expressive face was pleading for understanding. "I'm sure that everything you're telling me is true. But it simply doesn't matter. I look at this program and I *know* which horse is going to win. There's nothing rational about it. It has nothing to do with dry tracks, nervous horses, or any other calculable condition."

She stared over his shoulder for a moment, gathering her thoughts. Her eyes were as level as her voice as she continued. "What it has to do with is Aunt Tillie and a special sensitivity, which I've apparently inherited. I know you're still skeptical," she said quickly as he opened his mouth. "Apparently we'll just have to agree to disagree. I can't follow your advice when all my instincts tell me to do otherwise."

Tactfully, she didn't remind him that so far her track record was better than his. "And, just to be fair, I won't expect you to change your lifelong pattern of gathering all the evidence, sifting through it and reaching a conclusion." Ignoring his dissatisfied expression, she asked, "*Now* will you place my bet on Harpsichord?"

"Under protest," he told her, reaching for her tickets.

"I'll walk along with you," she said. "It'll be a while before the next race."

"You really don't enjoy this, do you?" he asked, sharply aware of her fleeting expressions.

"No." She shook her head. "I think a lot of the fun is the anticipation and excitement. The unknown. Screaming and shouting to encourage your horse, then feeling clever because you guessed right. But there's no anticipation for me. It's a bit like reading a mystery after someone told me that the butler did it."

He laced his fingers through hers, his voice quiet with conviction. "It's luck, Kara. Phenomenal, admittedly, but just luck."

Obviously she hadn't made a believer of him. Yet. "Ah, Logan, you're a hard man to convince," she said breezily. "Are you always this stubborn?"

His voice was level. "Always. And I'm even worse when I want something."

"Well," she said briskly, "if it's a winner you're after, you'd better bet on Harpsichord." She tugged at his hand. "Come on, the one part I do enjoy is collecting my money."

Twenty minutes later, she bit back a smile as Harpsichord crossed the finish line a neck ahead of Dane's choice.

In the next race, they actually selected the same horse. "Surprise, surprise," Kara said. "Why did you choose her?"

"Because everything indicates that she should win. Why did you?"

"Because I *know* she's going to win," Kara said, trying not to sound smug.

"You're just learning to figure the odds, and you're too ornery to admit it."

"Me? Ornery? It must be the company I'm keeping. I've always been compliant, agreeable, oozing the spirit of goodwill from every pore, a veritable vessel of ungrudging—"

Dane halted, turned her to face him and met her smiling lips with his own. "And you talk a lot, too," he murmured, when he finally lifted his head. Ignoring the people rushing by to place their bets, he held Kara close, watching as her expression of dazed pleasure turned to one of wrath.

"Dane Logan! If you think—"

He steered her back to their seats, his deep voice overriding hers. "I don't think; I know. You can't hide your response to me. You shiver when I touch you, and I can feel the explosion when we kiss. You're too damn stubborn to admit it, but it's there. As usual, though, it's neither the time nor the place to settle the issue. But soon, damn soon, we'll find a place where your walls aren't falling in on us, where your aunt and dead uncle aren't sending cryptic messages, and where we aren't surrounded by a crowd like this. Then we'll do something about it."

Kara sat down, moodily reflecting that he was right. Why couldn't the good-natured Terry have caused even a mild stir of excitement in her? Or any of the other men she had dated over the years? Why did it have to be this one? Why a man who was driven crazy by her impulsive nature and was quietly determined to change her?

She stared at the track, absently noting that their horse was two lengths ahead. And just what did he mean, "We'll do something about it"? She shook her head. No way, Mr. Logan. That would lead to nothing but a lot of trouble.

What had ever happened to her vow to avoid him? she wondered. Then she remembered. *He* had happened to it. He had taken over, telling her when he would pick her up and where they would go. Soon, she promised herself, she would learn how to get one step ahead of him and stay there.

His voice interrupted her silent declaration. "Should we go get our money?"

Dane's brows rose questioningly as she nodded, flashed him a sunny smile and walked lightly beside him. He looked down at her, wondering what dire plots were running through her head. She was far too agreeable for his peace of mind.

Two hours later, Dane drove the Porsche out of the parking lot. Kara upended her bag and filled her lap with bills of various denominations.

"Where do you want to stash your loot?" he inquired.

"Would you mind driving to the shop? I can put it in the safe. Besides, there are a couple of things I want to take care of," she said absently.

"I thought it was your day off?"

"It is, but I was kept busy out in front this week, and I have to finish some things in my workroom. My gosh! I've got twenty-seven hundred dollars!"

"I know," he said dryly.

"Now I don't have to go to Caliente next week. I'll just take the money down instead."

"Then the day wasn't a total loss. I can't think of anything more frustrating than watching your method of picking one winner after another, but it was worth it to keep you away from Caliente."

"Not a method," she corrected, ignoring the rest of his statement. "Intuition."

He muttered something that sounded like "Arrgh!"

"Still not convinced?"

"No."

It's a good thing he's a good loser, Kara thought. Because he'd lost a bundle. They had spent the rest of the afternoon disagreeing over which horses would win. She had never realized that there were so many variables involved in betting. He had concisely explained each one, bet his money and promptly lost it. He was persistent, she had to give him that. He never lost confidence in either his knowledge or his evaluations. Too bad they didn't work.

By some miracle Dane found a parking place within walking distance. He would have known it was her shop even without the six massive ferns doing sentry duty by the outside windows. The half-round, scalloped awnings were sparkling white, flanked by lacy, white wrought-iron railings. Hanging baskets of fuchsias supplied brilliant splashes of color. It was feminine and very classy. A distinctive sign above the door read CACHET.

Next door was a large, outdoor flower shop, overflowing with luxuriant shade plants of all varieties. Kara exchanged waves with Gary, the owner. Dane recognized the man from the Business Association charity dinner. If he remembered correctly, Kara had offered him another home-cooked meal. He idly wondered how long it would take to edge all those hungry men out of her life.

"Come on, I want you to meet Judy and Beth." Kara slipped her arm impulsively through his as they stepped through the door.

Beth's eyes widened as she took in Dane's lean, masculine grace as he towered over Kara. "Judy's in the office," she informed them, blinking as Dane acknowledged the introduction. Her lips pursed in a silent whistle as she turned and watched them walk away.

Judy looked up as the door opened. Her blue eyes were bright with interest as Dane nodded politely, for all the world as if she were someone's maiden aunt, she thought, then returned his shimmering gaze to Kara's animated face.

Judy looked absolutely gorgeous, Kara decided. Her black hair was pulled back in a glistening knot, the severe style enhancing her high cheekbones and expressive eyes. Just the sophisticated type to attract Dane. It was only fair to give Judy a chance with him, she thought virtuously.

After they had chatted idly for a few minutes Kara made her move. "I have to do some things in the workroom. It'll take me about an hour." Reaching for the doorknob, she turned back casually. "Judy, how about offering Dane some coffee and entertaining him for a while?"

Dane was on his feet before Judy could open her mouth. "I noticed that you were doing your book-keeping when we interrupted you," he said, looking down at her. "I won't take up any more of your time. I'm sure we'll see each other again soon." They exchanged amused smiles and two sets of expectant eyes returned to Kara.

"I'll just follow along with you," he said evenly. "I'm interested in seeing your workroom."

Kara cast a fuming glance at her partner and led Dane into the narrow hall. She ignored the sound of muffled laughter coming from behind the closed door.

Swinging open the next door, she turned on the lights and waved Dane in. His astonished gaze swept the room, then settled on her face. "This is *your* workroom?"

"I kept trying to tell you that I wasn't completely helpless, but you wouldn't listen. Who do you think does all the display work around here? How do you suppose I manage to work with glass and other mediums without some knowledge of tools?"

Dane wandered over to a pegboard-lined wall. A businesslike array of tools, clamps and brushes was neatly held in place by hooks.

"What's this?" He flexed an unusual pair of grips.

"Grozing pliers. You're in my stained-glass section. They're used to trim away jagged edges and to shape pieces of glass for better fitting." She moved to his side and pointed to various items. "Circle cutter, spring clamps, glass cutters, glazing hammer and double-bladed shears. I'm sure you're familiar with the rest of the stuff."

He examined various types of pliers, then moved a few feet away to look at hammers and saws and a case containing a supply of nails, screws and hooks, all organized by size. He raised his brows at the sight of an acetylene torch.

A cabinet for paper covered most of the next wall. He opened drawers and found that the supply ranged from mat board to rainbow-hued tissue. He glanced at boxes of paint, brushes, a couple of easels and a large workbench along the remaining walls. A drawing board and stool stood in the center of the room.

"So this is your domain." His voice was thoughtful. She was perched on the stool, and he stood beside her, looking down at a design that was taking shape.

"This is it," she said matter-of-factly. "I think I mentioned that Judy runs the business side. I hold up the artistic end. The only problem is our business is doing so well that I spend less time over there—" she pointed to the workbench "—and more here at the board. Without intending to, I seem to have moved into designing."

He watched as her hand moved swiftly over the paper. "How did that come about?"

"When we opened I made most of the handcrafted items. And I'm not talking about crocheted booties," she explained dryly. "Most were individualized art objects: stained-glass windows, skylights, hanging lamps, woven wall hangings, things like that. Soon I couldn't keep up with the demand. People around here want original accessories for their homes. I don't just mean different; they want the one-of-a-kind sort of thing. They're willing to pay well, but I couldn't keep up with the orders."

His eyes followed her slim fingers as she brushed back a strand of hair that had fallen over one eye. "Soon I was haunting the art department at the university looking for talent. God knows, there's enough of it around. So now," she grinned suddenly, "I guess you could say that I'm a contractor, too."

Dane pulled up a stool beside her and straddled it. Apparently there was no end to the surprises she had in store for him. At their first meeting, he remembered, he had dismissed her as a youngster. A sassy, annoying, provocative bit of jailbait. The next time he saw her he had all but fallen out of the window as she walked through the door in that cotton-candy dress. When he took her home and all hell broke loose at the front door, he had decided that, although she needed a keeper, he wanted and intended to have her.

Of course, there were extenuating circumstances. Anyone who coped with a charmingly spacy aunt and a chatty, defunct uncle could be allowed a few eccentricities. But it was not a fetching bit of fluff who had assumed responsibility for a rapidly growing orphanage and who worked so efficiently in this room. No, this was a many-faceted lady. And she was his. She hadn't realized it yet, and probably wouldn't admit it when she did, but she was his. And he couldn't wait to learn what other surprises were waiting for him.

Dane leaned over and kissed a tempting spot on her nape that he had been eyeing for the last five minutes. "I'm going to browse around your shop," he decided. "Don't rush on my account, honey. Take as long as you need."

Kara looked at the closing door in bemusement. *Honey?* He seemed to be saying that a lot lately, and she didn't think he used endearments lightly. It also seemed that he was taking a lot for granted. Absently rubbing a tingling spot on her nape, she returned to her drawing.

An hour later, she locked the door and walked to the front of the shop. Dane was leaning on the counter, returning his wallet to his hip pocket, talking to Beth. They both looked pleased with themselves. Very pleased.

Kara drew to a halt before Dane. Before she could utter a word, he asked, "Ready to go?" At her nod, he smiled at the younger girl behind the counter. "It was nice meeting you, Beth. Thanks again."

She nodded and murmured, "My pleasure."

Once Kara was in the car, seat belt buckled, she frowned in suspicion. "Thanks for what?"

"Hmmm?"

"Don't try to look so innocent. You can't carry it off. You and Beth. What are you up to?"

He drove the short distance to her house in silence. It wasn't until he opened her front door that he answered her.

"Bribery and collusion."

"What?"

"I paid her to work for you tomorrow, and she agreed to do it."

"Don't you think you should have consulted me?"

He wasn't deceived by her mild tone. "I could have," he agreed. "But you would have argued and confused the issue. As it stands, it works out beautifully. Beth needed the extra money, and I wanted us to have more time together."

Her eyes darkened with indignation, and she drew herself up as high as her sixty-three inches would allow. "Did you stop to think that I might have plans of my own?"

"Since you expected to be working all day, no."

"Look, this may come as a shock to you, but I don't need a social director. I'm twenty-five, not fifteen—" She ignored his murmured, "Thank God for small favors," and plowed on. "I've been making my own arrangements, planning my own life for some time now, and I can't imagine why all of a sudden you think that I need you to organize my every waking moment."

He moved to the striped sofa and sat down. "And sleeping."

She almost overlooked the quiet comment. Almost, but not quite.

"What?"

"You heard me," he said evenly. "I told you the first night we went to dinner that I wanted you sleeping in my bed. I don't want you to forget it."

"I don't even think about it," she said, lying through her teeth. She shot a quick glance at the big man sitting with rocklike patience across from her. Why me? she reflected. All she asked out of life was an ordinary man, pleasant, uncomplicated and agreeable, with a sense of humor. And what did she get? None of the above.

In all fairness, though, she had to admit that his sense of humor was developing. When they first met he had been in a state of unrelenting grimness. Now he actually smiled. Every now and then.

"I'm going to have to teach you to enjoy life," she said, unconsciously verbalizing her thoughts.

"Fair enough," he agreed promptly. "And I'll teach you to enjoy love."

"How do you know I don't?"

"Honey, as skittish as you are, you've either been sadly neglected or abused. And you don't have the look of someone who's been mistreated."

She eyed his bland face suspiciously. Was he laughing at her again? Blast the man! He might be lacking some of the traits she considered desirable, but he had enough self-possession for a regiment!

Kara sighed audibly. "Why," she asked a spot on the ceiling, "can't men be satisfied with a simple relationship?"

"The simpler it is, the better a man likes it," Dane explained to the same spot, shaking his head sadly at her lack of understanding. "Nothing pleases him more than a relationship reduced to its bare necessities."

Kara rose, giggling despite herself. "I give up."

He reached out a hand, snagged her wrist and tumbled her into his lap. "Good. That saves a lot of time."

She snatched her hand away and poked at his chest with a slim finger. "Look," she said, forcing herself to meet that shimmering green gaze head-on, "you might as well get this straight. We are not going to be lovers. I sleep in my bed; you sleep in yours. That's the way it is and that's the way it stays."

"Wrong," he contradicted deliberately, confiscating her hand and placing a kiss on the prodding finger. "We'll be lovers before the month is over. You'll be in my bed, your bare body curled against mine, wondering what all the fuss was about."

"You're so sure of yourself," she whispered, momentarily shaken by his statement. "Maybe that act works with other women," she said finally, rallying, "but not with me."

"There *are* no other women, not now. And it's no act." His fingers laced in the silvery silkiness of her hair, cradling her head as he lowered his. His lips were just a whisper away, his gaze locked with hers, when he stopped.

"Just as there hasn't been another man for you. Ever. Isn't that so, Kara?" He watched intently as awareness flickered reluctantly to life in her dreamy dark eyes. "Isn't it?" he insisted.

Her pupils narrowed, warning him too late as she twisted lithely, slid out of his arms and scooted to the end of the couch with more haste than grace. "You pick the damnedest times to ask questions," she complained lightly. She could feel the heat in her cheeks and wondered if he would believe it was due to exertion.

"I thought not," he said with satisfaction, ignoring her words. "But I want to hear you say it. Tell me, Kara. Tell me there's been no other man."

"You really do take the prize for rudeness, you know that, Dane?" Her eyes sparkled with anger.

His voice was sharp with impatience. "Rudeness be damned. I want an answer."

"You are the most infuriating man I've ever known!" she shouted, glaring at his inflexible face. "All right! If it's so important! I've never slept with a man! And as long as we're setting the record straight, if and when I do, it won't be with you!"

"The hell it won't."

His words were soft now, but they hadn't lost any of their determination. His sudden grin surprised her. "Face it, my Lady Moonlight, we have an appointment with destiny—in my bed—before the month is over."

The words forming in Kara's mind were shattered by the ringing of the telephone. She slid from the couch, saying, "How much do you want to bet it's Aunt Tillie offering to be a chaperone?"

"Hello." She shot a triumphant glance at Dane. "Hi, Aunt Tillie. Yes, he's here."

Dane groaned, and Kara's smile grew wider.

It faded abruptly as she listened. "You've got plumbing problems," she informed him. "Your pipe in the master bathroom has sprung a leak, and the water's on its way into the bedroom. Aunt Tillie's getting a bit vague here. Says it's heading toward something big and round."

"My bed," he muttered, standing and checking his pocket for his car keys.

"Thanks, Aunt Tillie. He's on his way." She replaced the receiver, saying, "You'd better hurry. She's worried about the big, round thi—your *bed?*"

"Right," he said tersely, heading for the door.

"You have a *round bed?*" she asked, relishing his harassed expression.

"Anything wrong with that?" he asked stoically. He'd break Tim's neck, he decided for the twentieth time. What was the use of having a friend in interior decorating if you couldn't trust him? He'd asked Tim to finish the bedroom while he was on a trip. And that's what he'd found when he'd come back.

"Not a thing. I've just never seen one. How do you

put sheets on?" It was an effort, but she remained straight-faced.

"Like any other bed," he said prosaically. "You start in one place and work your way around." He'd almost sent it back, he remembered. But it didn't look bad, and it was comfortable. That was all he required from a bed.

"Well, if I had any doubts before, they're gone now. I wouldn't be caught dead in a round bed."

His hands rested on her shoulders, and he drew her close for a quick, hard kiss. "You'll be very much alive," he assured her. "And I'll guarantee one thing. Before the night is over you won't know or care what shape bed you're in."

Kara glared at his retreating back until the door slammed behind him. Then her expression slowly changed. A satisfied smile curved her lips, and she laughed softly. She wondered when Dane would realize that he had neither questioned nor scoffed at Tillie's call. She'd give a lot to see the expression on his face when he remembered how he'd automatically reached for his keys and headed for the door.

Chapter Seven

"You mean Dane's gone? No warning or anything? Just disappeared?" Judy asked in amazement.

"Not quite." Kara curled up comfortably in the large wicker chair across the desk from her partner. "He called yesterday. Said there was some trouble on a construction site somewhere and he had to go straighten it out. Can't you just picture it?" she asked dreamily. "He'll be down there snapping out orders to someone other than me, peering over someone else's shoulder for a change, finding fault with—what?"

"I said," Judy repeated patiently, "where is 'down there'?"

Kara waved her hand in a vaguely southern direction. "Brazil."

"Good grief!"

"Or maybe it was Bolivia. I'm not sure."

"Well, they *are* right next to each other," Judy

mocked gently. "It's easy to understand why you'd be confused."

"Or it might have been both," Kara continued. "All I know is that he'll be gone for a while. Do you realize that it will take him a day to get there and a day to get back? And if I'm lucky, he'll find some awful mess that'll keep him occupied for a week or ten days. Two weeks!" she enthused. "Two whole weeks—"

"Kara."

"—without him telling me to lock my doors—"

"Kara."

"—without him scowling every time I mention Tijuana—"

"Kara."

"What?"

"Aren't you going to miss him?"

"Miss him? *Miss* him? Are you crazy?" Her look of amazement seriously tested Judy's self-control.

"Not even a little?"

"There's no such thing as 'a little' anything with Dane. From our very first meeting he's hovered over me like a hawk, telling me what to do, what not to do and how to do what he *allows* me to do. If you think I'm going to miss that kind of smothering, you're sadly mistaken. Nuts. *Crazy.*"

"All right! Sorry I asked."

Kara sat up straight. "I have, if all goes well, two weeks of freedom staring me in the face. Two weeks of being able to finish a telephone conversation without him interrupting. Two weeks of going down to see the kids without an armed escort. Two weeks of absolute, total, complete and unrestricted freedom! And you ask if I'm going to miss him?"

"Silly of me," Judy murmured dryly.

Kara stared in suspicion at her friend's bland face. "Very," she finally agreed. "You know what I'm going to do while he's gone?" she asked, staring vaguely over Judy's head. Not waiting for an answer, she continued, "I'm going to enjoy some nice, long baths, knowing that he won't be pounding on the door. I'm going to see friends that I haven't seen since he's had me in isolation. I'm going to talk to the men he's hustled me by and scowled at for the last few weeks. I may even have time to finish designing the stained-glass window I've been trying to work on."

Judy nodded agreeably. "Sounds fascinating. That should keep you busy. Tell me if you can make room in that crowded schedule to have dinner with your partner some evening."

"Sounds terrific. As a matter of fact, let's do it tonight. Are you in the mood for quiche?" At Judy's nod, she rose. "Let's meet at Jon's at seven," she said, referring to one of their favorite restaurants.

For the rest of the day Kara locked herself in her workroom. She completed a drawing for a wall hanging of a quetzal, a colorful, crested bird of Central America. She taped it to the wall and moved slowly around the room, checking the design from all angles. Yes, that should satisfy Mrs. Moreton's passion for exotic birds.

After squinting one last time at the drawing, she picked up the telephone and dialed. "Eddy? This is Kara. You can pick up the bird. What? Yes, I have sample colors. Just remember to keep the greens brilliant. This is going to be the focal point of the room. Okay, see you later."

Scratching the quetzal off her mental list of things to be done, Kara returned to the drawing board and was soon immersed in a wrought-iron gate, subtly entwining the family initials into the scrollwork. Her rumbling stomach eventually broke her concentration. Mildly surprised to find that it was four-thirty and that she had skipped lunch, she added one final touch, put her supplies away and went home.

The telephone began ringing as she pulled out her key. Muttering darkly as she fought with the two locks, she flung open the door and raced for the telephone.

"Hi, Aunt Tillie," she gasped.

"Hello, Kara, dear. You didn't have to hurry. I knew you were on the way."

"It's that second lock. I'm still not used to—oh, my God!"

"What's the matter?"

"I knew it was you," Kara gasped in astonishment.

"Of course you did," Tillie agreed.

"You don't understand. I *knew* it was *you*." Kara's dark eyes were wide with wonder.

"Is this the first time it's happened?" her aunt asked after a moment.

"First? You mean it'll happen again?" Kara demanded in a weak voice.

"It's another step, Kara." Tillie's voice was warm with understanding.

"Well, I don't like it. I want it to stop right now! It's getting altogether too spooky!"

Her aunt sighed philosophically. "It's lonely, too. But you've already learned that. And there aren't too many people you can share it with. But you learn to cope. And, if you're flexible, you manage to help people by keeping one jump ahead of things."

Kara's voice grew quiet. "Is that why you're calling, Aunt Tillie?"

"What do you mean?"

"Are you keeping ahead of things? Are you warning me about something?"

Tillie's voice was once again light. "Walter does all the warning these days. Such a busy man."

Kara waited patiently for her aunt to come to the point.

"He did want me to mention something to you."

Kara remained silent, waiting.

"But he's getting quite cryptic," Tillie complained. "It's most annoying."

"What did he say, Aunt Tillie?"

"To follow your feelings."

"Follow my *what?*"

"Feelings, feelings!"

"Sounds like something out of a musical," Kara grumbled. "Just what am I supposed to do with that profound bit of advice?"

"Think about it," her aunt suggested. "By the way, say hello to Dane for me."

"He's out of town," Kara said absently, brooding over her aunt's words.

"I know, but he'll be calling. Give him my love."

Kara gingerly replaced the receiver and backed away from it as if it were a strange dog baring its teeth. "I don't want to take another step," she informed it firmly. "Picking a winner at the races is one thing; looking into the future is altogether different. I don't want—"

She yelped in surprise as the telephone rang again. Lunging forward, she lifted the receiver and tentatively held it to her ear. "Hello?"

"Kara? Is anything wrong? You sound odd." Her partner's concerned voice was soft in her ear.

"Judy? Thank God!"

"Something *is* wrong. What is it?"

"Nothing now. Because I didn't know it was you."

"And it would have been bad if you *had* known?"

"Awful! But now I know that Aunt Tillie was just a coincidence, not another step."

"Well, of course," Judy said, her voice quivering with amusement. "How obvious. Kara, why is having a conversation with you always like running a circular obstacle course? There are lots of hurdles, but no beginning or end."

"Well, I know what I'm talking about," Kara said reasonably. "That's really all that matters."

"I'm not going to get involved in one of your convoluted discussions right now," Judy said firmly. "I called to see if we're still meeting for dinner."

"Of course. Why wouldn't we be?"

"No reason at all. But the last time we tried this, you forgot and stood me up."

"You're right," Kara admitted. "But nothing, neither rain nor shine nor sleet nor hail will make me late tonight. I'll be there at seven on the dot."

Spurred on by her promise, she dropped the receiver and headed for her bedroom. After spreading a white sleeveless dress on her bed she moved into the bathroom and turned both faucets on. Glancing at her watch, she decided that she had time for one of those much discussed long baths. She poured in some floral-scented crystals and watched as the water first frothed creamily, then blossomed into large, sparkling bubbles.

Kara trotted into the kitchen and poured herself a large glass of iced tea. Walking back through the living room, she collected an art magazine she'd bought earlier that day. She deposited those two items on the edge of the tub, then returned to the bedroom, picked up the cordless telephone and set it beside the tub. Within seconds she had shed her clothes.

"Ahhh." She eased back and cocooned herself in fragrant water up to her neck. Baths were absolutely, delightfully, decadently sinful, she decided. With a bit of concentrated effort, she just might be able to direct all her affairs from the tub. Just think! A tray spanning the top could hold food to stave off hunger pangs; a telephone could be her connection to the outside world; and a good book at hand would aid her escape from that same world when it became too hectic.

She closed her eyes and contemplated her water-logged future with a drowsy smile. It probably had some drawbacks. She'd have to ask Dane, she thought with a yawn. He'd undoubtedly come up with a solid dozen or so without even blinking an eye.

The shrill ringing of the telephone roused her. Groping over the side of the tub with a damp hand, she noted sleepily that most of the water had trickled down the drain.

"Hello," she said huskily.

"Kara?" There was no mistaking the deep voice. He could have been in the next room.

"Dane? Where on earth are you?"

"Rio de Janeiro."

"What time is it?" she asked in a panic.

"A little after eleven."

"*What?*" She sat up abruptly. "Judy's going to murder me! I was supposed to meet her at seven!"

His chuckle was a soft, totally masculine sound. "Relax. We're five hours ahead of you. You'll make it."

"I still have to get dressed," she informed him.

"What are you wearing?"

She looked down at herself. "Bubbles," she said honestly.

"*What?* Just where the hell are you going?"

It didn't take a psychic to know where his mind was wandering, she thought with indignation. "I'm wearing bubbles now because I'm getting out of the bathtub. In a few minutes I'll have on a dress that would satisfy even your puritan outlook. Besides," she added belatedly, remembering that they had a few things to discuss, "it's none of your business what I wear."

"We're going to have a long talk about that when I get home," he said firmly.

"We certainly are!"

"But in the meantime," he said emphatically, "all you have to do is remember that it *is* my business. Everything about you is my business. What you wear, what you don't wear, what you do—everything!"

"Now hold on just a damn minute," she snapped.

"In case you haven't figured this out, I own myself. I belong to me and no one else!"

"Honey," he said with a grim certainty that took her breath away, "the first night we went to dinner the pink slip changed hands."

Kara was silent, wondering how the sound of this man's voice could make her dizzy with rage while, at the same time, warming her with an unfamiliar sense of security.

"Is there some real purpose to this call?" she finally asked with asperity.

Damned if I know, he thought in atypical confusion. I'm calling because I'm thousands of miles away and, for the first time in my life, homesick. Because I can't hold you in my arms and feel your body curve against mine as if it were made for that very purpose. Because hearing the sound of your voice is as necessary as breathing.

He raked his hands through his shower-damp hair and listened to himself say, "I suppose not. I'm about to crawl into a very large, very empty bed." His words grew slow and emphatic. "I'm tired of large, empty beds. That's another thing we're going to talk about when I get back."

Closing his eyes in disgust, he wondered what it was about Kara that brought out a heretofore unknown streak of raw possessiveness in him. And that made him come across as a rampant male chauvinist every time he opened his mouth.

"I'm not responsible for the condition of your bed," she reminded him. "I'm sure you can remedy the situation any time you like."

He changed the subject abruptly. "How are your

. . . uh . . . bubbles doing?" He pictured her petite form clad in nothing but froth and was aware of the dull ache of his own body.

Kara looked down with a clinical eye. "Popping," she said succinctly. She grinned at the sound of a smothered oath. Served him right for asking, she thought.

"Kara?" His voice was husky when it broke the long silence.

"Yes?"

". . . Nothing." The pause that followed puzzled her. "Just . . . Kara."

He was definitely acting peculiar, she decided. He wasn't commanding or demanding. If she hadn't known better, she'd almost have said that he was uncertain.

"Promise me something?"

"If I can," she answered cautiously.

"Don't do anything harebrained. If you have to get into trouble, at least wait until I get back."

There! Now he was back to normal! "I don't plan on doing anything you'd disapprove of," she said sedately.

She heard an unconvinced grunt before he told her to enjoy her dinner with Judy and hung up.

Kara reached for a towel and patted her body until she was dry and bubble-free. What she had said was the truth, she told herself virtuously. He automatically took a dim view of most of her actions, but if he didn't know what she was up to, he couldn't disapprove. Right? Right!

But what was it about his voice that had her antennae quivering? Could he actually have sounded lonely? She shook her head as she stepped into panties and hooked her bra. Impossible. Not Dane Logan. The white dress slid over her head, and she occupied herself with the buttons. The diversion didn't help.

She knew lonely when she heard it and, unfortunately for her, she believed she had just heard it. Kara did not kid herself. She knew only too well her propensity for bringing home strays. Her family had learned to react with aplomb when they rose in the morning and found temporarily displaced friends sleeping on the living-room sofa. They recognized the fact that Kara could no more walk away from an emotional appeal than she could an injured child. It was a highly inconvenient but inherent part of her character.

Kara grabbed her purse, tussled once again with the double locks and told herself bracingly, "It can't be that. He probably drank the wrong water and is coming down with Montezuma's revenge." The thought bouyed her spirits so much that Judy eyed her with suspicion all through a lively dinner.

Five days later, pacing the length and breadth of her workroom, Kara wasn't so sure. In fact, she was wrestling with some alarming questions.

Dane called every evening. It was almost spooky, she decided. Her schedule varied each day but, with unerring instinct, he timed his calls to perfection. Shortly after she walked through the door, and long before she was due to leave for the evening, the telephone rang. The conversation was casual, rambling and costly. When she pointed this out he replied that he was unwinding after a long, hard day. Besides, he could afford it. He ignored her comment that he could accomplish the same thing and save a bundle by taking a long walk.

It was those conversations that were making her so uneasy. They were so unlike Dane, so . . . chatty! He discussed his progress in Brazil, talked about his family, asked about her day at the shop. She had learned more about him in the last few days than in all the times they had seen each other before he left. He was being too amiable, too . . . everything! She had never regarded herself as suspicious, but she trusted this new persona less than she did the old, familiar autocratic one.

Once, last night, he had slid back into the old mold. He'd commented that she would soon be living with him. She had reminded him, once again, that in her life, bed and board trotted hand in hand with love and marriage. It was his reply that had her pacing so restlessly.

His voice had been deep and quiet. "Don't you think I know that?"

When she failed to respond, he had said, "Good night, sweetheart. Think about it."

Think about it? How could she do anything else? On the other hand, how could she even consider it? This was the same man who had hauled her into his truck and proceeded to reorganize her nicely jumbled life-style, wasn't it? Indeed it was!

It *was* the same man who drove her to distraction with his logical and analytical approach to life, wasn't it? Absolutely!

The very same man who had expressed his unflattering opinions in a loud and clear voice when her intuition ruled her actions? Once again, yes!

She had known from the very beginning that he was nothing but trouble. Right? Right!

She had decided that the less she saw of him, the better it would be for all concerned. Right? Right!

And now that he was gone she had proved it. Right?

When no answer was forthcoming she tried again. Right?

Well, an inward voice that sounded suspiciously like her own was saying, I'm not too sure about that. This week was supposed to be fun, but I thought it was a bit flat. I missed having the hulk around, spicing things up. He adds a bit of a challenge to life.

Those other men are nice, but don't you think they're a bit *too* nice? I'm tired of men who smile all the time. And, you have to admit, the conversation gets a bit dull with no one to play devil's advocate. Yes, yes, I know. He *tells*, not asks. He's impatient and entirely too outspoken. But, even so, *I* think he has definite possibilities.

Kara perched on her stool, a dazed look on her face. Good Lord, she informed herself with horror, I *miss* the man.

Chapter Eight

"Kara, for heaven's sake, will you please sit down and tell me what's bothering you!" Judy's exasperated words finally penetrated the haze around Kara. Troubled dark eyes slowly rose to meet blue ones bright with speculation.

Kara stopped pacing and dropped obediently into the wicker chair. "Judy," she asked slowly, "have you ever had the feeling that something is wrong, but you can't figure out what it is? You look around and everyone seems to be okay, but you have this gut feeling that something's going to happen?"

"You know that I have to see black clouds, lightning bolts and raindrops before I realize that a storm is coming," Judy said lightly. "You're the psychic around here."

Moving swiftly at the fleeting look of panic that crossed her friend's expressive face, Judy knelt and laid her hands on Kara's. "You're serious about this, aren't you?"

Kara nodded.

"And frightened, I think."

Kara hesitated, then nodded again.

"And you're freezing," Judy scolded, attempting to conceal her shock. "Should I turn off the air conditioning?"

"Heavens no," Kara said lightly, trying to erase the worried frown from Judy's forehead. "We'd be roasting in minutes."

Judy perched on the corner of the desk. "Have you talked to Aunt Tillie about it?"

"Don't ask."

"Bad?"

"Only if you call it bad to know that she started out the same way I did, with horses. And that over the years, with no help or encouragement, she became what she is now."

"That's not bad, it's awful."

"If you're interested," Kara joked feebly, "I can tell you exactly how a sense of impending doom feels."

"Thanks, but I'll pass." Judy sat quietly, eyeing her partner. "It is interesting, though." At Kara's indignant look, she added hastily, "Academically speaking, of course."

"Of course."

There was a profound silence while they thought.

"Look at it this way," Judy said finally. "You can't identify the problem, but maybe you know what it *isn't*."

"Huh?"

"Humor me," Judy said. "For instance, is it Dane?"

Kara shook her head. "No, he's okay," she said positively. Dane was another problem, she thought. One she could worry about later. He probably wouldn't be home for another week, and she would have time to sort out her feelings before then.

"We're making progress," Judy said briskly. "Let's handle this just as we would any other problem, using the process of elimination."

Kara grinned involuntarily at her friend's business-like approach.

"You've got . . . uh . . . strong feelings about something, but it isn't Dane. Right?"

Kara drew a shaky breath, aware that they were both avoiding the word "premonition." It didn't alter the situation, but it brought some small measure of comfort. "Right."

"Does it seem to involve the shop or any of us here?"

"No." Kara dragged out the word thoughtfully.

"Your house? Aunt Tillie?"

Kara shook her head.

"Your parents?"

"No."

Judy's next words were tentative. "The orphanage?"

Kara drew in a sharp breath and closed her eyes. "Bull's-eye," she said faintly.

"Oh, Lord, I'm afraid to ask anything else."

"It wouldn't do any good," Kara sighed. "I don't *know* anything. I just have this awful feeling that . . ."

"That what?"

"That something's going to happen," she repeated helplessly. "And what makes it worse, Uncle Walter's been sending me mysterious messages."

Judy's brows rose with interest. "Despite my penchant for the strong, silent type, that man fascinates me. He's never at a loss for words. What are the latest ones?"

"I'm to follow my feelings."

"I beg your pardon?"

"Don't get cute. You heard me."

"Sounds like a song I heard on the radio yesterday. Something about a sweet little gal who missed her la-ast cha-ance because she didn't follow—"

"Please! Spare me the Tin-Pan-Alley bit. With Uncle Walter going enigmatic on me, the last thing I need is for you to break into a song and dance."

"Sorry." Judy grinned unrepentantly and moved back to her chair. "So what are you going to do about it?"

"What can I do?"

Judy gestured vaguely. "Something concrete. All you're doing now is worrying that you're getting as telepathic as your scatty relatives. How about calling Juanito and asking how everyone is?"

"They don't have a phone, remember?"

"Oh, yeah. Well, you have a car. It wouldn't take thirty minutes to get there."

Kara brightened, then drooped visibly. "It wouldn't be fair to take off and leave you with everything here."

"Just how much help do you think you've been these last few days?" Judy asked with the candor of long friendship. "You've paced and muttered and scared customers away. Business will probably pick up as soon as you leave. Our accountant will love you, and I give you my blessing."

Her last words were delivered to Kara's back as she went through the door. "But remember," she called, "if your massive protector comes around unexpectedly, I didn't suggest the trip. In fact, I know nothing about it!"

Kara chuckled, grabbed her purse and trotted out the front door. It felt so *good* to be doing something. It might not be the right thing, but it was action.

An hour later, she was on her way. She had made a special purchase at a large department store, packed some clothes, told her next-door neighbor that she might be gone a couple of days and called Dane's house to leave a message on his machine. She even remembered to make the customary stop for additional car insurance before she crossed the border.

If Dane found out about this, he'd murder her, she thought, dodging a spirited driver who had decided that her side of the road looked more inviting than his own. But she'd be back long before he returned, and there was no reason for him to know, she assured herself. Anyway, she was still a free agent, wasn't she? He might have adopted an annoying attitude of ownership, but she certainly didn't have to validate it by allowing him to get away with it.

Maybe the secret was to be more assertive. All she had to do was inform him—tactfully, of course—that she still retained the right to run her own life. That seeing him occasionally did not mean she had handed herself to him on a platter. He would listen, agree and back off.

Like hell he would! He bulldozed right over tact, subtlety and any other gentle quality. Besides, she realized with shock, she didn't exactly want him backing off. At least, not permanently. Pondering her own inconsistent nature, she turned the green Camaro through the open gate into the yard.

As usual, children came running from all directions, shouting greetings. The noise brought Carmella to the porch. After Kara had dispensed kisses and hugs, she turned to the other woman with a questioning look. "Fifteen?"

"*Sí*, God has been good to us." Observing Kara's pensive gaze, she asked, "Is something troubling you, my friend?"

"Funny, that's what I came to ask you." She moved restlessly, looking out over the dirt yard to the vegetable garden. "Carmella, is there anything wrong down here? Anything at all?"

"No." The other woman's voice was serene. "We are all well. But it seems that things are not the same with you. Where is your man?"

"Brazil," Kara said shortly. She was tempted to explain once again that Dane wasn't hers, but gave it up as a lost cause.

Carmella smiled, relieved that the solution was so simple. "You will feel better when he returns," she assured Kara. "Come inside and we will talk."

That evening at dinner Kara mentioned that she planned to stay for a day or so. The meal immediately took on a festive note, and the girls were elated when she told them that she would be sleeping in their dormitory. After the children were in bed she sat on the porch with Juanito and Carmella. They talked softly, looking up at a dark blanket of sky studded with gleaming stars. Laughing as a huge yawn overtook her, she said a soft good night, tiptoed into the room and closed her eyes as soon as her head touched the pillow.

Her sleep was deep, but not restful. She was on a ship in the midst of a wild storm. Dane stomped around the deck bellowing like Captain Ahab. The ship lurched to one side as a roar seemed to rise from the bowels of the ocean. The scream of the wind was deafening.

"Carina! Carina!" Hands plucked at her shoulders and patted her cheeks. "Wake up. *Terremoto!*" The words were accompanied by a series of agitated cries.

Kara sat up, wide awake. She didn't need to speak the language to know that she was in the middle of an earthquake. And not a small one, either, judging from the grating rumble deep within the earth and the rolling motion of the floor. It was just past dawn, and gray light filtered into the room. Thank God we can see, was her first thought. Earthquakes were terrifying at any time, but fumbling around in the dark while beams creaked and groaned was nightmare material.

"Elena." She motioned to the girl who spoke the most English. "Everyone to the door." She gestured frantically. "To the door. Now!"

Shoes, they should put on their shoes, she thought. Bits and pieces of remembered information from an earthquake-preparedness class were running through her head.

While Elena relayed the instructions and herded

the girls to the doorway, Kara snatched the jeans, knit shirt and running shoes that she had dropped at the foot of her bed the night before. Later, if there was any broken glass or other damage, she could come back in and forage for the girls.

Juanito's voice boomed from across the yard. "Kara! Are you and the girls all right?"

"Yes," she called, trying to steady her voice. "Stay where you are. We're okay." Kara squatted down and held out her arms. Two trembling girls with tear-streaked faces immediately filled them. She held them close, feeling the frantic beating of their hearts against her body as the floor moved beneath their feet.

"Elena, tell the girls to move close to me. Now, put your arms around each other and stay right here. This can't last forever." She smiled encouragingly, wincing at the sound of breaking glass. Thirty seconds, she thought incredulously. It probably hadn't been any longer than that, and it seemed like an eternity.

They all jumped as a beam crashed to the floor and plaster dust covered them. The little ones wailed as the older girls shrieked. "Elena," Kara commanded, "tell them to stay right here with me. No one is to move until I say so." She wished she felt as sure of herself as she sounded. She also wished she had another set of arms so she could reach out to the rest of the frightened girls. But more than anything she wished for Dane.

It wouldn't matter if she set the feminist movement back ten years: She would gladly wave the white flag if she could be in his arms right now. He emanated such strength and determination that she always felt safe with him. Always would. Intellectually she knew that he couldn't do any more about an earthquake than she could, but wrapped in his arms she wouldn't care. Hell of a time to realize it, she thought ruefully, dodging another chunk of plaster.

Dane Logan, you'd better get yourself back here. And you'd better be quick about it. At the rate things are happening, I may not live long enough to tell you that I love you.

Kara was so stunned by the revelation that it took her a few moments to realize that the ground had stopped shaking.

"Come on, kids. Hold hands and follow me." She led them carefully around a tilting scrub oak into the center of the yard. "Stay right here. I'm going back to put on my clothes." She tugged at the cotton shirt she had slept in, remembering that it had been designed for comfort, not modesty.

She waved and retreated to the doorway as Juanito herded the boys outside. "We're all fine," she called. "Be with you in a minute. I'm going to get dressed." Nodding, she acknowledged his caution not to enter the building.

As she stepped into her jeans, her mind returned to the thought that was fully as cataclysmic as the earthquake. She was in love with Dane! How on earth had it happened? And just when, with all her evasive maneuvers and defensive tactics, had her heart realized that it belonged to a large, determined and rather too serious man? After tying her shoes, she straightened up with a grin on her face.

What fun it was going to be! The first thing she had to do was convince him that what he wanted in that ridiculous round bed was a *wife*. And, judging from some of his comments lately, that might not be too difficult. Then they could spend the next fifty or sixty years driving each other crazy. She contemplated their future with a wry expression. He would dedicate himself to tempering her impulsive nature, and she would do her utmost to lighten him up. Good heavens, the crazy man had a dimple that was almost extinct from lack of use!

Thinking about the delights ahead, she turned to survey the dormitory. It looked as if a bad-tempered giant had upended it. Cautiously, she stepped over the threshold.

Might as well grab some clothes for the girls as long as she was there. She looked up through a gaping hole in the ceiling and noted that the sky was turning blue. Her gaze shifted to the right. Several beams were angled suspiciously. No matter. On a day like today, with miraculous discoveries canceling out nature's temper tantrum, nothing could happen to her. She was invulnerable. She was superhuman, able to leap tall buildings with a single bound, to hold up a rickety room with one hand, to fly at the speed of light. She was . . . she was in love!

Suiting prosaic action to delirious ravings, Kara spread a blanket on the floor. She moved carefully, opening drawers and dumping their contents on the blanket. She was nearing the center of the room when the floor shifted beneath her feet. An aftershock! Any Californian knew that aftershocks were common and could be as dangerous as the original quake. Cursing her stupidity, she leaped for the door.

The room shuddered as the powerful rolling motion of the second quake increased. Kara was tossed to the floor. Clear-sighted, and well aware of her danger, she was no longer feeling euphoric. She felt more like someone had doused her with a bucket of cold water. If I die now, she thought in despair, he'll never know that I loved him.

Dimly, she heard Juanito bellowing her name. But the more ominous sound of a beam cracking over her head demanded her immediate attention. As if watching a slow-motion film, she stood in frozen fascination as the wood sagged drunkenly and fell. Finally moving her gaze from the awesome sight, she took one quick look around and dived between two of the beds that had been shuffled like a deck of cards and left almost touching.

She landed awkwardly and felt a sharp pain on the left side of her face, followed by one on the back of her head. After that, there was only the blessed darkness of oblivion.

Early Saturday afternoon, Dane slammed his front door and dropped his suitcase. He walked directly to a small table and poked a button on his answering machine. His phenomenal run of luck with the telephone had ended abruptly three days ago. It had been that long since he had talked to Kara.

Her husky voice riveted his attention to the machine. "Hi, Dane. It's Wednesday afternoon and I just wanted to let you know I'll be away on business for a few days."

"And why the hell couldn't you have told me about it the last time we talked so I wouldn't worry for seventy-two hours straight?" His mutter overrode her voice, and he had to replay the rest of the message.

Her voice was dry as she said, "To answer the question you're undoubtedly asking, I didn't say anything last night when we talked because I didn't know about it. I'll call you when I get back. 'Bye."

He shut off the machine, turned on the air conditioning and headed for the shower. Eyes closed, he stood letting the cool water stream over his head and down his heated body. She had to be the most aggravating woman in the world. He had crammed five days' work into three and gone without sleep for the last twenty-four hours, all because he couldn't get her on the telephone.

He lathered his hair with shampoo and rubbed briskly. If that wasn't bad enough, he'd heard about Thursday morning's earthquake and had visions of her body beneath broken beams and rubble. He hadn't relaxed until he'd heard that the epicenter was sixty miles south of Tijuana. The San Diego area had felt the impact, but there was minimal damage north of the border.

He froze, staring at the shower head, then swore as shampoo stung his eyes. Tijuana? She wouldn't have gone down there without him. Would she? Hell, yes! Had she done anything besides complicate his life since the moment they met? If disaster and chaos were to be found, would she be anywhere but right in the middle of it?

A minute later, a large towel tied around his lean hips, water still running down his back, Dane was back at the answering machine. His expression was grim as he played back Kara's message and waited for the next one.

Tillie's voice, rigid with control, was almost unrecognizable. "Dane? Please come and see me as soon as you can. Kara needs you."

Twenty minutes later he sprinted up the front steps of the frame house. Tillie opened the door and stepped into his arms. After a moment a shuddering sigh escaped her, and she raised her head from his chest. "It's not as bad as I thought." Her smile was strained, but his knees weakened with relief at the sight of it.

He closed the door, following her into the living room.

"I called you Wednesday evening," she said.

"The night before the quake?"

Tillie nodded.

"She's down there." It was a statement, not a question.

"Yes. She's hurt."

Dane paled beneath his tan. His lips were stiff as he asked, "How bad?"

"I don't know. I never know for sure. I only see bits and pieces." Her eyes were shadowed. "There was blood on her face and the back of her head."

Dane jerked as if she had hit him. He sat down next to her and took her small hand in his. Clearing his throat, he urged, "Go on."

She blinked away tears and sternly controlled her voice. "I didn't know if she was alive or dead."

Dane looked down at Tillie and marveled at her resilience. She had aged in the short time he had been away. And no wonder, he thought, accepting for the first time without question the burden that she carried. He would have turned gray overnight if he'd lived with such a nightmare.

"But you know now." Again it was a statement.

"Yes." Her clear eyes evaded his. "Walter told me that she's better."

Dane raised her hand to his mouth and kissed it softly. If she needed Walter, she could have Walter. And without any questions or comments from Dane. God only knew what sort of a support team *he'd* need if he were in her shoes.

"Well," he said, "I suppose I better go pick her up."

She brightened and rose, leading him toward the door. "Yes, dear, I think you should."

He looked down and realized that he had the doorknob in his hand. Had had it there since he walked in. Shrugging, he dropped it in the beribboned basket and leaned down to kiss Tillie good-bye.

"Oh! I almost forgot. Walter said there was something you should know."

"What's that?" Dane asked tolerantly.

"It doesn't sound like him at all," she dithered.

"What did he say?"

"He was very specific. I was to tell you that today, Saturday, Kara was going to be in hot water."

"Hot water?" Dane repeated blankly.

Tillie nodded. "That's what he said."

"Well, that's nothing new," he commented, starting out the door. She's always in—" He stopped as if he had run into a wall. *"Hot water?"*

Tillie nodded again, alarmed at the changing expression on Dane's face.

"She wouldn't do it," he stated with grim certainty.

"Do what?" Tillie asked in apprehension.

"Yes, she would," he snarled. "Tillie, so help me

God, if that niece of yours is alive when I find her, I'm going to murder her!" He looked down at her puzzled expression. *"Aqua Caliente* means hot water. She's at that damned racetrack today!" He turned without another word.

"Dane?" Tillie called tentatively after him.

"What?" He bit off the word.

"I wasn't going to say anything about this, because Walter *has* been acting peculiar lately, but—"

He turned, towering over her. "What?" he asked, too gently.

"It sounds so . . . well, so biblical," she said apologetically. "He said that a child would lead you."

He repeated blankly, "A child will—"

"—lead you." She nodded.

He swore softly, inventively and with great feeling. "Tillie, I'm going to find her, drag her back by her silvery hair and—"

"Marry her?" she asked hopefully.

"If I don't throttle her first." He glanced at his watch. "The races started an hour ago. God only knows what she's been up to in that time."

"You'll take care of her," Tillie said with satisfaction.

"You can count on that. I can hardly wait to get my hands on her," he said with grim anticipation as he loped to the truck.

Chapter Nine

Two hours before Dane entered the shower, Kara was arguing with Juanito.

"No," he said adamantly, folding his arms across his chest and glaring at her.

"Why not? It's a perfect opportunity and you know it! They've checked the racetrack with a magnifying glass and a fine-tooth comb and declared it safe for tourists. Our bandit friends will be busy propping up their homes. We need more money to rebuild this place. It's the perfect time."

"No."

"Why not?"

"Dane will not like it."

"Who cares? We were doing this before he came along and we'll keep right on."

He shifted uncomfortably, but held his ground. "He will not like it," he repeated stubbornly.

"Are you going to let him intimidate you?" she challenged.

"Yes," he said simply.

She eyed him appraisingly. "Why? You're bigger than he is."

"It is not the size."

"Then what is it?"

"Something within here." He tapped his chest. "I have not his . . ."

"Killer instinct," she supplied dryly, ending his search for words.

"Yes." His voice was hopeful. "Now do you see why we cannot do this?"

"No. Dane's ability to go for the jugular has nothing to do with it."

"Kara, my brave little friend, Thursday we pulled you out of the building. We thought you were dead. When we saw that you were alive you slept so soundly that we were still afraid. The doctor told us how to care for you. Carmella and I, we sat up with you, praying that you would open your eyes and be well."

"And so I am," she said softly, noting once again that the formality of his speech was in direct proportion to his heightened emotional state.

He touched a gentle finger to her swollen cheek and looked doubtful.

She winced. "I know. I have a shiner to end them all, but time will take care of that." She turned and looked across the yard, where blankets were stretched over ropes to provide shelter from the sun. Most of the main house was undamaged, but the two dormitories, added at a later time and built with inferior materials, had been destroyed.

"And speaking of time, we don't have an awful lot of it. The kids can't live in this tent city forever. What if it rains? We have to get some money to rebuild."

Kara tapped her foot impatiently. So much time had already been lost. Too much. She had slept, intermittently, until Friday morning. She had opened her eyes to see Carmella's anxious face hovering over her. The doctor, on his visit, had left precise instructions. Carmella, attempting to follow them, had asked one question.

"Juanito," she shrieked a moment later, for once shaken from her normal serenity, "bring the doctor. She tells me she leaps tall buildings."

Juanito had roared off in his truck. Kara brooded fuzzily, then decided that she did indeed know her own name and that she just hadn't been given enough time to answer the question. She attempted to explain, but found that it was hard to talk when your head hurt, and went back to sleep. Later, a doctor awakened her and annoyed her enormously by shining a light in her eyes and asking rapid, incomprehensible questions.

"Juanito," she had said with asperity, "having a house fall on my head did not improve my Spanish. What does the man want?"

The doctor had left, muttering about rest, liquids and aspirin. She had been fed, cosseted and told to sleep. This morning she had risen, dressed and defied anyone to mention returning to bed. And now they had things to do, and this stubborn mountain of a man wouldn't budge.

"All right," she said in exasperation, "we won't go." She waited just long enough for relief to spread across Juanito's face before she added softly, "But *I* will."

The argument was fierce and loud. The outcome was a surprise to no one.

"Dane will slit my throat," Juanito announced. "He will slice me up and throw the pieces to the dogs."

"No, you'll probably get off with a few choice words. He'll be saving the big stuff for me," Kara said blithely. "You're still worried about those guys who chased me, aren't you?"

He nodded gloomily.

"Wait right here. I've got something I want to show you."

She ducked into the house. When she returned several minutes later he was talking to Carmella, protesting and gesturing expansively.

"What do you think? Will I pass for a native?"

Juanito stared down at her, speechless. She twirled around, a gleaming mass of black hair spilling around her shoulders. "I bought it before I came down. No one will even look twice at me." She twirled again and caught the wig as it tilted over one eye. "Of course, I'll fix it so it stays on."

"You think no one will look at a woman with a green and purple face?" he asked carefully.

"Oh, that. Even if they do, they won't connect me with the blond *gringa* who knows how to pick all the winners. They'll just think that you know how to keep your woman in line." She grinned up at the gentle man.

Carmella laughed. "You might as well go and do it. I'll stay here with the little ones. Why don't you let the older ones ride in with you? I don't want them playing around the fallen buildings."

Juanito asked, "Do you think they will be safe while we are inside?"

She nodded. "Tell them to stay together and sit in the shade until you come out."

Thirty minutes later, the truck pulled into the huge parking lot. The eight children obediently clustered in a shady spot and promised not to move. Kara and Juanito paid for their tickets, walked up stairs shaded by a green-and-white canopy and entered the massive stone building. They bought a program, found seats in the grandstand and plotted their strategy.

"Let's make bigger bets this time," Kara suggested after taking a hasty peek at the program. She had wondered if a crack on the skull would negate her peculiar skill, but apparently it hadn't. The names still leaped out at her like neon lights.

She jabbed Juanito with her elbow. "Will you stop that? You're making me nervous, peering over your shoulder as if you expect the devil himself to appear."

"I think he is already here," he muttered. "See? To our right, four rows behind us?"

Kara turned casually, gazing in the direction he had indicated. Every seat was full. "Who am I looking for?" she whispered.

"The dark one, with the mustache."

She darted a quick glance at him to see if he was kidding. He wasn't. She wondered if it would be tactless to inform him that all the men looked dark to her. And that those who weren't bearded all seemed to have mustaches. She was pondering this bit of international courtesy when he spoke again.

"He was one of those who chased you that day."

"What!" She spun to face him, automatically adjusting her wig. "Are you sure?"

He nodded.

She frowned in concentration. It was one thing to convince her friends that the pursuing men would never recognize her. It was a horse of another color to be four rows away from one of them in a wig that tilted and slid at the slightest provocation.

"We'd better separate," Kara said decisively. "One lone giant is less conspicuous than a giant with a midget. Our friend just might happen to remember you. And that bit of success might spur him on to recall that the midget you were with last time was blonde. Let's use our divide and conquer routine and hope it's more successful this time."

She circled the names of the winning horses and handed the program to Juanito. "You take this and stay by the cashier's window, somewhere near the center. Don't come back. If you bet all the winnings of each race on the next one, you should have plenty of money by the fourth or fifth race."

She shushed him as he began to protest. "Just listen for a minute. Once you're gone, I'll blend in with the rest of the crowd. No one will pay any attention to me. I'll meet you by the window after the fifth race. If we have enough, we'll leave. Okay?"

He nodded reluctantly and rose.

It was a perfect plan, and it should have worked. It *would* have worked, Kara maintained later, if it hadn't been for the two men behind her. No, to be fair, it really began with the wig. It was hot and uncomfortable. So much so that she loosened some of the pins and surreptitiously slid a finger under it in an effort to scratch her sweaty scalp. Her head began to throb, and she thought longingly of a cool drink and a nap. Only two races to go, thank God.

The men behind her had devised a game to relieve the tedium between races. It consisted of whacking each other—and any hapless bystander—with rolled newspapers. That, combined with the heat and the noise of the crowd, was almost more than Kara could bear.

At the end of the fourth race she stood and stretched. The men behind her had resumed their jousting and whacking. Then things happened so quickly that only later could Kara recall the sequence of events. First, a tug on her wig. One of the men had lunged and tangled his paper weapon with a long strand of her dark hair. Then two yelps, one of pain from her, one of surprise from the man, as her wig was whipped from her head and sailed through the air like a large, hairy spider. There was a scream of pure terror as it landed in a woman's lap, then a roar of surprised laughter.

A breeze cooled Kara's overheated scalp. Her first comfortable moment of the afternoon was spoiled when her eyes met those of a man four rows up and to her right. A gold tooth glittered as he smiled in triumph.

When the fifth race began Kara quietly edged out of her seat and walked down the stairs. Before she reached the bottom she was encircled by men, all equally dark and mustachioed.

She heard a roar from the crowd and knew the race was almost over. Looking down, she saw Juanito turn to the cashier's window.

"This way, *señorita*," a quiet voice said, urging her toward the exit. Her protest went unvoiced when something sharp touched the small of her back.

Her circle of abductors herded her down the stairs and outside into the hot afternoon air. It was absolutely the last straw, Kara thought wretchedly. Her headache had escalated from a dull throb to lancing pains. The only thing in the world she wanted was a hard bed and a soft pillow. Instead, she had a knife in her back and a handful of hairy men.

The men seemed to be arguing about something, but Kara spied the waiting children and her attention was focused on them. They glanced up, caught sight of her and left the shade of the tree. They stopped, looked for Juanito and turned back to Kara in confusion when they couldn't find him. She shook her head, willing them to stay away.

Ruben, the oldest, spoke rapidly to the others. They separated and formed a loose semicircle around Kara and the men. The men paid no attention to the ragtag group of children.

Elena positioned herself as close to Kara as she could. Kara asked a man in a blue, sweat-stained T-shirt, "Where are you taking me?" The men ignored her, but their argument grew loud and vehement. The children listened and looked at each other.

Elena tossed a stone to Benito and called, "What do you think we should do now?"

Kara closed her eyes in relief. Bless those little

streetwise kids! They were clearly waiting for instructions. Trying to ignore her pounding head, she thought. Finally she turned to a man in a green, sweat-stained T-shirt and said distinctly, "Wherever you take me, my friends will follow. They will find the big man I was with, and he will come and get me." The men ignored her, as usual, but she noticed that, after a conference with Elena, Miguel and his little brother, Luís, disappeared.

Feeling a bit like the pied piper, Kara, still surrounded by men and followed by children, was hustled out to the parking lot. She was led to an ancient, rickety truck with fully bald tires. At the thought of enduring a ride in the decrepit, probably springless wreck, Kara discovered within herself a wellspring of defiance.

She dug in her heels and said, "No!"

The men stopped in surprise and repeated, "No?"

"No!"

Just as the men looked prepared to lift her bodily and toss her into the cab, Kara heard the sound of a familiar motor. Juanito's truck, with Ruben at the wheel, bore down on them. Ruben, Kara recalled, had an affinity with all things mechanical. He had even managed to teach her to hot wire a car.

Her captors froze in horror as Ruben apparently lost control of the large vehicle. As one man, they shouted "No!"

That was the last word Kara understood for some time. Juanito's runaway truck came to a stop by skidding into the other one and locking bumpers. The men jumped out of the way, pulling Kara with them.

Then they exploded into sound, apparently shouting five varieties of the same thing. It took a long time for them to adequately express their feelings.

Ruben looked contrite and willing to be helpful. He remained behind the wheel, ready to follow orders. Kara remained with a man in a bright red shirt while Green, Blue, Gold Tooth and Sombrero jumped on the bumper of their truck to lower the front end. When they were satisfied they shouted vigorous instructions and motioned for Ruben to back up. He nodded, shifted gears with hideous grating sound and bolted forward.

The men flew upward in wildly balletic leaps, then plummeted to the ground. Kara winced at the thuds and the expressive comments that followed. Ruben shrugged apologetically and pointed to the steering column. He was commanded to leave Juanito's truck and mount the bumper of the other one. He was joined by Blue, Gold Tooth and Sombrero, while Green replaced him behind the wheel.

The three men bent, then straightened their knees, shifting their weight. Kara was reminded fleetingly of a folk-dance step, but it soon became apparent that they knew what they were doing. The nose of the truck lowered, then rose, with their shifting weight. When it dipped low enough Juanito's truck could be put in reverse.

Ruben finally seemed to understand the process, but had a lamentable lack of rhythm. He bobbed up as they bent down, then reversed the procedure. The three men glowered and grumbled, and finally one of them pushed him to the ground.

Kara watched as the children milled around, always

moving, looking as if they were involved in a game. Elena caught Benito's elbow, gesturing to a nearby tree. She boosted him up until he could reach the lowest limb. He disappeared behind the dusty leaves, and all Kara could see was the agitated jiggle of a red balloon. He soon emerged, handed the balloon down to Elena and jumped to the ground.

With a grinding sound from the bumpers, a roar of Juanito's motor and a screech of tires, the trucks were separated. The children shouted and surrounded the vehicles. As a festive note, Elena tied the red balloon to the antenna of the antique truck.

Kara was sandwiched between Sombrero and Red Shirt in the cab. The remaining three vaulted into the bed of the truck. She craned her neck as they pulled out of the parking lot. Ruben was busily deploying the troops. He gestured for Alberto to remain behind and urged Benito, Carmen, María, Oscar and Elena into the truck. He jumped behind the wheel and slowly followed the bobbing balloon.

Juanito pocketed his money and turned away from the cashier. It was more than enough. Now all he had to do was collect Kara and leave. If they were lucky, Dane would never know of this particular trip. He moved aside and leaned against a pillar, scanning the crowd. A shaft of light beaming down from a window near the exit caught his eye. It shone on a woman's silvery hair, reminding him of Kara. He remained still, knowing that she would quickly spot him. Far more easily than he could find a small woman with dark hair.

He stood patiently, a smile curving his lips as he

remembered the day he had met Kara. Old Serefino had thought he was dealing with a lunatic. She wanted a plant stand but, even consulting a dictionary, had requested a plaster table. Serephino waved his arms and muttered about *gringas* who came to the wrong shop, wasting a man's precious time. Plaster tables? Who, he wondered aloud, made such atrocities? And who, in the name of God, would want one?

Later, after Juanito had explained and Kara had smiled, Serefino worried. How, he asked, did the little silver-haired one survive? She could not *talk*. Ten words, at the most, were all that she could say. And half of them were numbers. What good was it, he asked, to know a number if you could not say anything about it? And, he concluded gloomily, she even confused *ten* for *God,* so that left her only eight. Watch over her, he had ordered. Along with your other little ones, take care of the silver-haired child.

And Juanito had tried. He still tried. But she could wrap him around her little finger. And Carmella just laughed. Trust Kara, she said. She is a special child of God. She will bring us joy as well as good fortune. And so far she had done exactly that.

The crowd thinned, and he realized that the next race was about to begin. She should have come by now. He gazed around anxiously, belatedly remembering the man in the grandstand. He glanced at an approaching couple and was transfixed by the sight of a wadded bundle of dark hair in the man's hand. The man shook it and made a teasing remark to the woman beside him just as Juanito's hand gripped his shoulder.

"Where did you get that?"

One quick look at Juanito's size and scowl erased the smile from the other man's face. He quickly explained. Juanito was running for the exit before he finished.

He found pandemonium at the bottom of the stairs. Miguel and little Luís were explaining to a uniformed guard why they had been caught sneaking into the building. The guard was just as loudly describing what would happen to them if they tried it again or if they didn't go away—immediately!

Juanito swept the boys up, muttered a hasty thanks to the guard and ducked around the corner. "Now, tell me."

"Cariña is with many men," Miguel said.

"Bad men," Luís nodded.

"They are taking her away."

"Far away."

"Which way were they going?" Juanito asked.

"To the parking lot."

"That way." Luís pointed.

"Come on!"

They ran to the parking lot and found Alberto talking earnestly to the driver of a taxi. "See," he said, "I told you they would come." He turned to Juanito. "He will take you to Cariña. But he wants much money. You have money?"

Juanito nodded, then caught himself. "I don't need him. I have the truck."

Alberto shook his head. "Ruben has the truck. He's following the men."

"Bad men," Luís said.

"Ruben doesn't drive," Juanito said. "And I have the keys."

"He started it without the key, and he made the crash look like an accident," Alberto said proudly.

"What crash?" Juanito asked with foreboding.

"He hit the other truck with yours and made the bumpers lock."

"Where is he now?" Juanito asked grimly, not sharing Alberto's appreciation.

"He went out that gate," Alberto pointed, "following the old truck with the red balloon."

"I won't ask," Juanito muttered, then immediately did. "You mean the men who took Kara were stupid enough to tie a balloon on the truck?"

"Stupid men," Luís said in satisfaction.

"Elena did that so they could see the truck from far away."

Alberto pointed a finger at the entranced cab driver. "He said that he used to drive race cars and that this one is fast. Oh, Ruben said if he turns off of the main road, he will leave Oscar or someone to show you the way."

Juanito bundled Manuel and Luís in the backseat and climbed in beside them. He was still talking to Alberto. "You stay here. I think Dane will come for Kara. If he does, go with him and tell him what you've told me. If he doesn't come, I'll be back for you."

The driver slid his angular length behind the wheel. "My name is Jaime," he said, rubbing his hands as if preparing for the Indy 500. "How fast do you want to go?"

"How fast *can* you go?" Juanito asked.

"I don't know."

"Find out."

With a shrill cry that sounded like the mating call of a coyote, Jaime took off. He spun through the gate and turned to the right, his tires barely touching the road. "The canyons are this way," he remarked conversationally.

"I know."

"How far do we go?"

"Until we see a truck or a child."

"How far are we behind them?"

"I forgot to ask."

Jaime turned to face them as he sped down the road. "Is this your woman we are chasing?"

"No, my friend's."

"He must be some friend."

Juanito nodded. "And she is some woman."

"Who are the men who have taken her?"

"Bad men," Luís said.

Jaime looked ahead and screeched to a halt.

"Why are we stopping?" Juanito asked.

"Over there," Jaime pointed. "A child."

"Not one of mine," Juanito said. "Keep going."

"How many do you have?" Jaime craned his neck to face Juanito.

"Children? Fifteen today. Maybe more tomorrow."

"Do you have the money to pay me?" Jaime asked in sudden suspicion, lifting his foot from the gas pedal.

"I do," Juanito assured him. "Pull over! That's one of mine." He poked his head out of the window. "Which way, Benito?"

"That way," he shrilled, pointing to a road that angled up into the hills."

"Good boy. Wait in the shade of that tree. If Dane comes, get in his truck and show him the way. If he doesn't, I'll be back for you."

Jaime skidded to a stop at the next crossroad when Elena popped out from behind a bush. She pointed, Juanito repeated his message and they sped on. They passed Carmen, Oscar and María. Each pointed the way and received the same message. Finally Jaime took a curve on two wheels and slammed on the brakes. He came to a halt ten inches behind Juanito's truck. "So soon?" he mourned.

Ruben was on his stomach, looking over the side of the road. He wiggled back and put his finger to his lips. "Shhh. They're down there. They took Cariña into that old shack."

"Have they hurt her?" Juanito whispered hoarsely.

Ruben shook his head. "I went down there, but they were just talking."

Kara felt as if she had been in the small, hot shack for hours. Red had taken her elbow and prodded her into a single room, bare except for a small table. She had taken one look at the broken windows and cobwebs draped artistically in the corners and turned back to the door. Blue, Green, Gold Tooth and Sombrero stood looking at her. Sombrero had a scar on his cheek and looked meaner, if possible, than the others.

"Does anyone have an aspirin?" she quavered.

In the silence that followed she had more than enough time to remember all the horror stories of white slavery and rape. She jumped as Blue spoke rapidly to the others. Her eyes widened as they all patted their shirt pockets and dug into their jeans. One by one, they shrugged their shoulders and shook their heads.

"I'm sorry, *señorita*. No aspirin." Blue held up a mangled cigarette with an inquiring look.

"Uh, no thanks." She cleared her throat. "I don't think it would help my head. I hurt it," she continued nervously, "in the earthquake. Were any of you hurt?"

Blue spoke again, and again the men shook their heads.

"Nice place you have here," she said chattily.

Blue didn't bother translating, and the men just stared at her.

"You know," she finally said, swallowing dryly, "you guys are scaring the hell out of me. I wish you'd just tell me what you want and get it over with."

Blue broke into a spate of words. When he finished the other four spoke, individually and all together. The noise made Kara's headache worse.

Blue turned back to her. "We don't want for you to be scared," he said apologetically. "We bring you here only to talk." At her look of incomprehension, he continued. "We have families," he explained. "But we have no work, and they are hungry. We need money."

"You're holding me for ransom?" she asked in amazement. Of all the things she had considered, she had never thought of that.

Red, Green, Gold Tooth and Sombrero crowded closer with questioning looks.

"Ransom?" Blue repeated, puzzled. *"Qué es ese?* What is that?"

"Money. *Dinero.*"

Blue was stunned. "We don't steal people! We just want your help."

Kara pressed her aching forehead with her fingers. "I don't have any jobs to offer you," she said in bewilderment.

"You have something better," Blue replied.

"I do?"

"Sometimes we get jobs at the track. We see you there with the big man. And always you win. That is what we want. To know the secret."

Chapter Ten

"The secret?" Kara repeated weakly. Good Lord above! Aunt Tillie had warned her that there'd be days like this.

"But first I will explain," Red decided. "I will tell you who we are. I will tell you all about our need. I have brought you to a hot, falling-down house and cannot even give you to drink. No wonder you have fear."

Kara opened her mouth, realized that she didn't know what to say and closed it again.

Red nodded his head and tapped his chest with a dusty forefinger. "I am Domingo," he said. Starting with Sombrero, he pointed to each of the men, naming them. "Trinidad, Pepe, Gabriel and Sancho."

Kara nodded four times, doubting that she would keep them straight if they changed positions. The men shuffled their feet.

"They have no English," Domingo explained. "I have some, but much is lacking."

"You're doing fine," Kara assured him. It was far better that they work this out with his English than her Spanish, such as it was.

"We are brothers," he stated, as if that explained everything.

Kara waited, then realized that it was her turn. "My gosh," she murmured, "are there any more of you at home?"

"No more brothers," Domingo answered her literally. "But we have five wives—one to each of us—and twenty-seven children."

"Good heavens!"

"The wives have fear because we have no work."

Kara nodded in understanding.

"We have fear because we have no work."

She nodded again.

"The children—"

"—have fear because you have no work?" she hazarded a guess.

"No, they have hunger."

Sudden tears came to Kara's eyes. "Oh, Domingo, I'm sorry."

"Please, not to cry," Domingo pleaded. "My wife, she cries. Trinidad's wife, she cries. Pepe's wife, she cries. And—"

"—Gabriel's and Sancho's wives, they cry," Kara finished.

He nodded gloomily. "Tears we have much of, but they do not make bread or bring work."

"How long has it been like this?" she asked.

He shrugged. "Too long. In the past, we worked.

Building houses. But now there is no money to pay for work."

Kara nodded. She remembered the low-income housing projects that the government had subsidized.

"Between us," he said proudly, gesturing to his brothers, "we make fine houses." Pointing to each one in turn, he elaborated. "He is *carpintero*, I am *fontanero*, a plumber, he makes the doors and windows, he puts bricks and he puts plaster. We are good workers, but now too many peoples are here to live, and are not much jobs."

Kara nodded again. She was only too familiar with the nightmarish population explosion in Mexico and the resulting astronomical unemployment rate.

"What if you had a house to build?" she asked curiously. "Would you stay away from Caliente and work?" She wondered if two dormitories were the equivalent of one house. After all, she and Juanito had two busted buildings and some money. These five men and their assorted skills might just be the ones to put Humpty-Dumpty together again. It seemed like a fair arrangement.

He nodded vigorously. *"Sí.* But one house would go up very fast. *Whoosh!"* He gestured widely to demonstrate how a house would appear overnight with the five of them working on it. "Then we would need to find another."

Kara hid her doubts. In this charming land of *mañana*, where people rarely seemed to consult a calendar, much less a clock, she had never seen anything go *whoosh*.

"So," Domingo said, as if concluding a successful debate, "that is why we need the secret."

For the first time Kara confronted all the ramifications of her dilemma. As Dane had told her ad nauseam, she could not save the world. The orphanage was a drop in the bucket, but these five men with their wives and twenty-seven children were opening the floodgates. If only her head would stop pounding, she thought optimistically, perhaps she could come up with a solution.

Leaning against the table, she rubbed her forehead. Domingo pulled a grubby handkerchief from his pocket, flicked the top layer of dust from the table and, with a gallant gesture, urged her to be seated. She sat and pondered the situation.

Five hopeful pairs of dark brown eyes followed her every move. She closed her eyes to shut out the sight. If only they weren't so nice! If they were the ordinary criminal type, she could be planning an escape. But instead she had to worry about them. Not only was she unable to help them financially, she had to protect them from Juanito's wrath. For, without a doubt, the kids had devised an ingenious rescue plan and soon her large friend would be barreling through the door breathing fire. She had never seen Juanito angry, but the sight was bound to be awesome.

One step at a time, she told herself. First explain about the "secret," then warn them that they were in imminent danger of having their necks separated from their shoulders.

"Domingo," she said carefully, "it's obvious that you and your brothers are proud men. You've worked hard all of your life, and you are not asking for charity."

He spoke briefly to the others, and they all nodded in agreement.

"I don't know how to tell you this," she said with effort. "But there is no secret."

"No secret?" Domingo asked, looking puzzled. "But, *señorita,* you never lose."

"That's right," she admitted reluctantly. "But I don't know how I win."

Looking as confused as she felt, Domingo relayed the information to his brothers. "They say you must know how you do it," he said, after listening to the four of them.

"But I don't," she repeated. "My aunt says it is a gift," she pointed up with a forefinger, "from God."

His eyes widened. "A gift?" He turned to the others excitedly. *"Un don de Dios!"*

The men looked up and, with a single reflex, crossed themselves. A thoughtful silence fell on the occupants of the shabby room. It was broken when Trinidad spoke at length to Domingo.

"My brother wants to know if you had done some wonderful thing to deserve this gift?"

Kara shook her head. "Not that I know of." She listened sleepily as an excited barrage of words erupted between the men.

Domingo's voice was taut with excitement when he asked his next question. "My brothers ask if you had changed your life in any way when this good fortune came to you?"

Kara opened her mouth to say an automatic no, closed it and gave the question some thought. "If I remember correctly," she said slowly, "I had just started meditating." She ignored the excited buzz of conversation between the brothers. "But I don't think *that* had anything—"

"Meditation is a way to speak to God, *verdad?*" Domingo asked.

"Well, I suppose it is," she admitted reluctantly. "But I just thought of it as clearing my mind, a way of relax—" Shrugging, she watched as the men turned to each other. They spoke loudly and at great length.

Domingo faced her. "We would like you to teach us to speak to God about the horses."

"But that's not the way it works," she protested. "I never mentioned horses to Him. Not even once. I don't think you understand."

"*Señorita,* I implore you. Teach us how you speak to God."

"You do that every time you pray," she reminded him.

"*Sí, sí,*" he said impatiently. "But we also want to learn your way."

"Domingo," she said sternly, "you don't bargain with God."

His look of reproach would have shamed a saint. "*Señorita,* would we do such a thing?"

"I don't know."

"We will not ask about horses," he promised finally, noting the stubborn look on her face. "But if He mentions them, we will listen!"

Kara giggled at the absurdity of the whole conversation. "That's fair enough."

"You will teach us?"

"If that's what you want."

"We want," Domingo stated firmly.

"All right." She gestured to the floor. "Gentlemen, have a seat."

"You're getting as weird as Tillie," Dane informed himself as he passed the first two gates of the Caliente parking lot. He should have parked, bought a ticket and torn the place apart until he found her. Instead, he was driving around the parking lot looking for a kid. He found Alberto swinging on the chain-link fence by the next gate.

"Dane!" Alberto almost tumbled off in his excitement. He scrambled into the truck and pointed. "That way. Hurry! Cariña has been gone for a long time! Why did you take so long?"

Dane squelched the impulse to utter a few pointed words. He'd save them for the proper person. "Is she all right? Was she hurt?"

"In the earthquake," Alberto said. "But that was a long time ago. Today was more exciting."

"Tell me about it," Dane suggested, preparing for the worst. Ten minutes later, as they were flying down the road, his face was dark with fury. He uttered a pithy phrase, then remained grimly silent.

"Look," Alberto pointed. "There's Benito!"

Dane slammed on the brakes, and the truck stopped in a cloud of dust.

"*Arriba*, Dane. *Arriba*!" Benito shouted, pointing up the steep road.

"Good boy," Dane said. "Get in, and let's go find her."

A few miles farther, Elena was waiting for them.

"*Arriba!*" she called, pointing up and to the right. They pulled her into the truck and roared up the steep incline.

Carmen dropped from a tree limb as they approached. She, too, pointed up.

"I know," Dane said. *"Arriba!"*

Carmen nodded, saw that the front of the truck was full and scrambled into the back.

Farther on Oscar, then María, ran to the side of the road, pointed the way and joined Carmen in the back of the truck.

Dane took the last curve with more speed than caution and came to a flying stop less than a foot behind a green taxi.

"What the hell?" Then he shrugged. A taxi on a dirt road miles from anywhere was merely one more oddity in this crazy situation.

Two men turned to inspect the new arrivals. If he hadn't been ready to strangle Juanito, Dane might have been amused at the blend of apprehension and relief on his face. "Thank God!" the big man said.

Dane joined them at the side of the road. "Where is she?"

Juanito silently pointed down to the shack.

"How long has she been there?"

"An hour, more or less."

Dane's voice was deadly. "Then what the hell are you doing up here?"

Jaime looked at the large, murderous man and whistled silently.

"Softly, my friend." Juanito touched Dane's arm. "They have not hurt her. Ruben watches from behind a bush. He tells us that all they do is talk."

"I don't give a damn what they're doing. I want her away from them."

Jaime turned to Dane. "Isn't that just what I have been telling the big one? We should run down the hill, shouting so we sound like many men, kick in the door and—"

"—and what are they doing while we shout and kick?" Juanito asked in disgust. "Sticking knives into her?"

Dane looked inquiringly at Juanito. "Who's he?" he asked, nodding at the bony man.

Juanito pointed silently at the taxi. "Jaime."

Dane closed his eyes. "I don't believe it. Of all the cab drivers in Tijuana, you get the one who wants to play cowboys and Indians!" He shifted impatiently. "Let's get Ruben up here," he snapped.

Ruben arrived, panting from the climb. "I can see everything through the window," he reported. "But they are doing nothing. The men sit on the floor and talk to Cariña."

"That's all?" Dane asked in disbelief.

Ruben nodded vigorously.

"How many windows are there?"

"Two. One across from the door and the one I've been watching through at the side."

"How many men?"

"Five."

Dane exchanged a look with Juanito. "Let's go. You take the side window and I'll get the door."

"What do you want me to do?" Ruben asked.

Dane hesitated, then looked at Juanito.

"He has done a man's job today," the big man said.

"Don't let them out of the back window," Dane told the boy.

"What about us?" The other children drew closer.

"You girls stay up here with Luís." At their disappointed murmur, he ordered briskly, "If the men get away from us, make sure they don't take the trucks."

"Can we throw rocks at them?" María asked.

"As many as you want," he said absently. "Benito, Oscar, you go with Ruben. When I give the signal, you make as much noise as you can."

"Wait a minute!" Jaime said to Juanito as they turned away. "What about me? Didn't I bring you here? Didn't I wait with you? Didn't I tell you how to save the *señorita*? Am I going to be left out now?"

They all turned to Dane.

He closed his eyes, a reluctant grin curving his lips. Why was it that everything involving Kara turned into a three-ring circus? "No," he said, suddenly cheerful, "you can come along and kick the door down. That will be the signal," he said to the younger boys. "Until then, not a sound."

Five minutes later, they were in position. For the first time in hours Dane's stomach muscles relaxed. As he passed the window, he had glimpsed Kara sitting cross-legged on the table. The men were sitting on the floor facing her. He had to admit that she didn't seem concerned.

"What's that funny noise?" Jaime whispered.

Dane shrugged. "Almost sounds like someone's got a stomach ache. You about ready?"

"Should I use my foot or my shoulder?" Jaime asked, suddenly realizing that knocking down a door might be more complicated than it looked in the movies.

Dane shrugged again. "You're the expert on doors."

"My shoulder," he said. "That way, I can get a running start."

A running start, he decided later, is undoubtedly helpful if a door is jammed or locked. But if the door in question is already ajar, it is unnecessary, if not excessive.

Kara's eyes rounded in pure astonishment as the rescue operation began. Yipping like a demented coyote, a tall, bony man burst through the door at a dead run, tripped over Pepe's crossed feet and catapulted through the window. Juanito stepped through the side window as a confused din broke out in back. Dane filled the doorway.

Kara flew to Dane, threw her arms around him and rested her head against his chest. Her words were inadequate, but straight from the heart. "Oh, Dane, I've wanted you so much."

His embrace threatened to crack her ribs. "Kara, don't you *ever* do this to me again! I've been so damned scared."

She raised her eyes to meet his and almost stopped breathing at his dawning expression of fury.

His fierce gaze took in the bruises on her face. He set her on her feet and steadied her. "I'm going to murder the bastards," he said, releasing her and turning to her abductors.

Kara grabbed at his shirt. "Dane, wait a minute! They didn't hurt me." She caught his arm, trying to pull him back. Touching her cheek, she explained, "This happened in the earthquake."

"And I suppose you'll tell me next that they didn't kidnap you?" His breathing was still ragged with surging adrenaline.

"No, they did that," she admitted reluctantly. "But they had a good reason."

"I can't wait to hear about it," he said in the taut voice of a man who wanted to lash out at someone. *Anyone.*

Juanito apparently shared his feeling, Kara noted. And his frustration. He had advanced on the five brothers and, one by one, hauled them erect. He no sooner had one upright and turned to the next when the first one toppled back to the floor. They were now, all five of them, sitting again, drumming their heels on the floor.

"What the hell is the matter with them?" Dane asked blankly, diverted momentarily from his plans of mayhem.

Kara swallowed, trying to vanquish the laughter that was bubbling in her throat. "I think their feet fell asleep."

"From what?"

"Sitting cross-legged."

She had his full attention now. "And why were they doing that?" he asked in a gentle tone that should have warned her.

She cleared her throat. "Because I was teaching them to meditate, and that's the way I learned."

"Damn it, Kara, enough is enough!" Dane's voice was a full-scale roar, momentarily overriding the war cries of Benito and Oscar, and the moans of Jaime as he sat outside in the dirt, clutching his aching head. "I am going to ask you a simple and direct question and I want a simple and direct answer. Just why were you sitting on a table in an abandoned shack in the middle of nowhere teaching five bandits to meditate?"

That's simple? she wondered as she murmured, "Brothers."

"What?"

"They're brothers, not bandits."

"I don't give a damn if they're quintuplets; answer my question!"

"Well," she said cautiously, "it started with Uncle Walter's message."

"Kara," he warned, "don't you dare start on one of your rambling stories. We're talking about bandits—brothers, whatever the hell they are."

"I know. I'll get there in just a minute. But if you're going to understand the whole thing, you have to know what led up to it, and it starts with Uncle Walter."

A spasm crossed Dane's face. He listened to her husky voice as she explained about her conversation with Tillie. Was he out of his mind? he wondered. He had rushed back from Rio because he didn't want another day to pass before he claimed her. He wanted her in his arms, in his bed, in his life. He needed her in ways that he had never needed another living soul. If his life was to have any meaning, it had to be shared with this sprite who, if given half a chance, could deprive him of his few remaining wits.

He drew her back into his arms, for the sheer pleasure of feeling her body melt against his, while he listened.

"But I knew you'd be worried if I came without you, so I got the wig to disguise myself."

"What wig?" he asked, fascinated despite himself.

"The black one," she repeated patiently. "So I'd look like everyone else down here. I'd show it to you, but the men behind me at the track knocked it off when they fought with the newspapers."

"These men, Kara," he said distinctly, pointing to the five who were slowly getting to their feet under Juanito's watchful eyes. "I want to hear about them."

"I'm getting to them," she assured him. "It was because of the earthquake. That's the only reason I went to the races. Otherwise the money I won at Del Mar would have lasted for a long time. But when the buildings collapsed—"

"With you in one of them," he said grimly.

"Uh, yes." Now was definitely not the time to tell him that she had gotten out safely, then deliberately gone back in, mooning like a lovesick adolescent. "Anyway, I told Juanito that we should get the money today so we could start rebuilding."

"And what did Juanito say?"

"That you wouldn't like it," she replied honestly.

He grunted. "Well, at least someone was using his head."

"But I convinced him we should go. Rebuilding is expensive, and that was the only way I knew to get it done."

"Damn it, Kara. Do you know how much money I have?"

"Well, not to the penny," she hedged. "But everyone knows that you're filthy rich."

"Didn't it ever occur to you to ask me for help?"

"Of course not," she said, horrified.

"Why the hell not? Everyone else does."

"But, Dane, the first time we met, you told me how you felt about that. You called me a patsy."

He could see that it still rankled.

"You said that your friends didn't ask for help and neither did you. You said that people had to quit leaning on others and take care of themselves. And maybe you're right—about some people. But not where the children are concerned," she said definitely. Her expression was earnest. "But you do see why I couldn't come to you, don't you?"

He nodded grimly. Yes, he understood. This exasperating love of his didn't realize that she was the one exception to the rule, to every rule. That she was the one person he would willingly pauper himself for.

"Anyway," Kara said, conscientiously returning to her narrative, "everything would have been fine if my wig hadn't flown away. Domingo saw my hair, and the next thing I knew, I was being escorted to the parking lot."

"Alberto told me what happened there. I want to know about what went on here."

"Darling, you should have seen the kids! They were so wonderful. And Ruben! Something has to be done for that boy, Dane. With his talent, he could become a world-class car thief, or a mechanical genius. What's the matter?" she asked, aware that he had been trying to stop her flow of words for some time.

His voice tense, he asked, "What did you call me?"

Kara felt as if she were drowning in his shimmering green eyes. "Darling?" she repeated faintly.

He drew her closer, and neither of them heard

Juanito's softly voiced words to the terrified brothers. Neither of them noticed the boys racing through the door, or that a moaning Jaime had poked his aching head back through the window.

"Kara, my love, will you answer a simple question?" He lifted her off her feet in an embrace that once again threatened her ribs.

"I haven't finished answering the first one yet," she whispered, brushing her lips across his cheek where his dimple would be if only he smiled more often.

He looked down at her. "Do you love me?"

"Of course I do!"

He almost dropped her. "Then why didn't you ever tell me?"

"You never asked me."

He looked astounded. "I didn't? Are you sure?"

"Positive," she said firmly. "From the day we met, you've been too busy telling me things to ask me anything. You've given me orders about the locks on my doors, orders about trips I will or will not take, orders about betting at the track, but never have you asked me anything of any importance."

She wiggled until her feet touched the ground. "Can we get question one out of the way, so we can concentrate on number two?"

He released her with obvious reluctance. "Where were we?" he asked in a distracted voice.

"I was coming into the shack with the brothers."

"Bandits," he muttered.

"Who's telling this story?" she demanded.

"I'm beginning to wonder if anyone is," he said with mounting impatience.

"First of all, and most important, they didn't hurt me. They've been perfect gentlemen."

"Except for abducting you," he said with justifiable sarcasm.

"Well," she admitted, "they did do that. But they had a reason."

"Do I get to hear about it?"

"Well, of course," she said in amazement. "That's what I'm trying to tell you. But you keep interrupting and bringing in all sorts of irrelevant matters."

She watched in fascination as a red flush mounted under his dark tan.

"Kara," he spoke with commendable restraint, "you have exactly one minute to tell me about the bandits."

"Thirty seconds will do it." She ignored his irritated snort. "But first, let's agree on what to call them. They're not bandits. They are five brothers. Brothers," she said slowly, easing into it, "who happen to be construction workers, but who are temporarily out of work.

"Brothers," she said in a rush, "who I am hiring to rebuild the dormitories."

She took a deep breath and held it, waiting for the explosion.

Chapter Eleven

It wasn't long in coming.

"Like hell you will!" he shouted over the noise of five voluble brothers, three whooping boys and one groaning cab driver. "I've put up with your aunt, your uncle, your antics at the racetrack and your bull-headed resistance to advice, but I'll be damned if I'll watch you hire a bunch of two-bit hoods to work at the orphanage. Think of the kids, for God's sake!"

"I am thinking of them." She did a swift sum in her head. "Forty-two of them."

Surprise rendered him silent for a moment. "I wasn't even gone for two weeks," he said in wonder. "How did they manage to get—"

"Juanito and Carmella just have fifteen," she clarified. "They—" she pointed to the brothers "—have twenty-seven."

"Does everyone this side of the border have an orphanage?" he asked bitterly.

"That's their family." At his disbelieving look, she nodded. "That's right. Each one has a wife, and between them they have twenty-seven children."

She turned the full blast of her beseeching eyes on him. "And they're hungry. Can you imagine what it's like to wake up in the morning knowing that you have no food for your children? No, I don't suppose you can," she added, answering her own question.

He couldn't bear to see the pensive look in her eyes. He had told her to face facts, to be realistic, but he hadn't known that reality would be so shattering. He hadn't known it would hurt so much when she realized that the line had to be drawn somewhere. That she couldn't make the world a safer, better place for everyone. He felt as if he had just taken deliberate aim and shot Tinkerbell.

"That's why they brought me here," she said, looking over his shoulder at a distant, sad place. "They thought that I could share some marvelous secret about the way I pick my horses. The winnings would tide them over until they found work again. And you know what? Suddenly I knew you were right. I had no secret of success to share, and I couldn't start taking them to the races, too."

She blinked and slowly focused on him. "I told them that I didn't know how to help them. I explained how the whole thing had happened to me, and somehow they latched on to the idea of meditation. When I said that I didn't think it had anything to do with the horses, they told me that they had no other hope."

Her eyes mirrored the sadness of those words, and suddenly he realized that whatever it took he wanted to see the sparkle return to her dark eyes, to bring back the animation to her expressive face. He wanted her ardently embracing a cause, even if it drove him crazy. He wanted her spilling over with enthusiasm and calling him darling again.

"Do you think they really know anything about building?" he asked mildly. Not that it mattered. He knew he was prepared to hire or train them, even if they were total incompetents.

"I don't know," she said absently, her mind elsewhere. "It sounded like it. Domingo said he was a plumber, and Gold Tooth is a carpenter. One lays bricks, one puts in doors and windows and one does plastering."

She shook her head reminiscently. "They were really determined to get the hang of meditating. Even if their legs fell asleep and their throats got sore."

"Oh, yeah," he remarked casually. "I heard that caterwauling."

"Caterwauling?" Indignant eyes met his.

"If you were teaching them to sing, you're going to have a problem. I think at least two of them are tone deaf."

"They weren't singing," she said protectively.

He was obviously relieved. "That's good. Because I noticed that they just sort of droned along, churning out the same note over and over."

Her back stiffened. "That just shows how much you know about meditating. They were repeating a mantra. And they were doing very well, too."

"To each his own," he said carelessly. "If they want

to sit on their backsides moaning while others are out working for a living, that's up to them, but I don't see how it's helping their kids."

"Moaning?" Kara prodded him in the chest with a slim finger. "Listen, you blockhead, if anyone has a right to moan, it would be those men! They've lived a hand-to-mouth existence for years. They've picked up odd jobs, looked for work when there was none to be found and somehow managed to keep their families together."

Dane leaned against the wall, arms crossed on his chest, his face expressionless. Only his eyes gleamed as he watched his furious little love stride back and forth as she castigated him.

"They weren't born with silver spoons in their mouths, like someone I could mention. But in spite of all they've faced they are persevering, patient and honorable men."

She veered to face him. "And you know what I'm going to do? I'm going to hire them! Without your approval or permission! We started this whole thing without you and if we have to we'll carry on the same way. First, they can rebuild the dormitories. When they're done with that we'll get them to do some of the other things that Juanito doesn't have time for. All I have to do is pay them." She faced Dane defiantly. "And we both know that I can get all the money I need."

Dane jerked as if the wall had suddenly become a sheet of flame. Spirit was one thing, but she was getting completely out of hand!

Kara spun on her heel and walked over to the group of gesticulating men. "Domingo?"

The men broke off an impassioned conversation and turned to her.

"Two buildings on Juanito's farm collapsed during the earthquake. Can you and your brothers build new ones?"

A smile split his face. "Sure, sure. We do everything." He tapped his chest. "I am *fontanero*," he reminded her. "He is—"

"I remember," she said hastily. "How much do you charge?"

"By the hour or the job?"

She looked frantically at Juanito.

"The job." Dane spoke from behind her in a clipped voice. "And I'll be supervising you every step of the way."

"Just a darn minute," she said, turning to glare at him.

"How much do you know about construction?" he demanded.

"Not much," she admitted.

Juanito spoke for the first time. "It is best this way, Kara."

"Good, that's taken care of," Dane said. He looked at Juanito. "If you'll make the arrangements with this talkative quintet, Kara and I have a few things to settle." He looked down at her mutinous face, clasped her hand in his and led her outside.

"I want to finish the interesting conversation we were having earlier," he said.

"About what?" she hedged.

"You told me that you loved me."

Direct and to the point, as usual, she thought in disgust. "I've changed my mind."

"Why?"

Hadn't he an ounce of tact or finesse? Talk about rough diamonds! "Can you give me one good reason why I shouldn't?" she demanded. "Why should I love a man who spends his time delivering orders and ultimatums? A man who always has a better way to do whatever I want to do? A man who has never had the decency to tell me that he loves me?"

His eyes shimmered with unspoken words.

"Do you love me?" she asked, deciding that his direct approach wasn't all that bad.

He shifted uneasily. "Can you think of any other reason why I'd put up with your peculiar uncle?"

"Do you love me?" she repeated.

"Or your aunt?"

"Do you love me?" she persevered.

"Do you think I make a habit of rescuing women and following them around to keep them out of trouble?"

"I haven't the foggiest idea. I'm asking a plain and simple question. I'd like an answer. Do you love me?"

"Damn it, Kara," he snarled in a most unloverlike way, "of course I do. And you know I do. Now are you satisfied?"

"Not quite," she said, watching with enjoyment as he squirmed. "A little tenderness might make it more convincing."

"I'm a little rusty," he admitted, as he bent his head and kissed her softly on the lips. "I've never said that to another woman."

"Good," she said promptly. "I'm glad to be the first, and I intend to be the last. Now that you've broken the ice, feel free to practice whenever I'm around. I'll need to hear it every now and then, and it'll sound better if I don't have to drag it out of you."

His mustache curved as he grinned. "Anything else?" he asked, as he wrapped his arms around her and drew her close. He groaned as her soft curves melted into his aching frame.

"Um-hmm," she whispered against his lips. "If we could get everyone out of here, we could go home and do some intensive practicing."

Reluctantly, he set her on her feet. "God, Kara, are we *ever* going to be alone?"

"Dane," she whispered, as Jaime staggered around the corner, groaning and holding his head, "who *is* that man?"

He laughed involuntarily. "Just someone who decided to join the rescue party."

"Does he have a job?"

A familiar frown replaced his smile. "Kara," he threatened, "don't start. In fact, before we go anywhere I want you to promise me something."

"What?" she asked cautiously.

"That you'll stop all this philanthropic nonsense, that you'll quit doing these harebrained, impulsive things and that you'll marry me."

Her smile blinded him as she flew into his arms. "Oh, Dane, more than anything else in the world I want to marry you!"

Later, with Kara still nestled in his arms, her lips still soft and sweet on his, it suddenly hit him. Oh, well, he decided philosophically, drawing her even closer to his taut frame, one out of three isn't bad.

READERS' COMMENTS ON SILHOUETTE ROMANCES:

"The best time of my day is when I put my children to bed at naptime and sit down to read a Silhouette Romance. Keep up the good work."

P.M.*, Allegan, MI

"I am very fond of the quality of your Silhouette Romances. They are so real. I have tried to read some of the other romances, but I always come back to Silhouette."

C.S., Mechanicsburg, PA

"I feel that Silhouette Books offer a wider choice and/or variety than any of the other romance books available."

R.R., Aberdeen, WA

"I have enjoyed reading Silhouette Romances for many years now. They are light and refreshing. You can always put yourself in the main characters' place, feeling alive and beautiful."

J.M.K., San Antonio, TX

"My boyfriend always teases me about Silhouette Books. He asks me, how's my love life and naturally I say terrific, but I tell him that there is always room for a little more romance from Silhouette."

F.N., Ontario, Canada

*names available on request